1920's Investigators' Companion

Equipment & Resources

H. P. LOVECRAFT 1890–1937

FOR THE 1920s
INVESTIGATORS' COMPANION

by

Keith Herber

with John Crowe

and Kenneth Faig Jr., Justin Hynes, Andrew Leman, Paul McConnell, Ann Merritt, Kevin Ross & Lucya Szachnowski

project leader and editorial **KEITH HERBER**
graphic design and layout **LES BROOKS**
production assistance **RYK STRONG**
cover design **CHARLIE KRANK**

CHAOSIUM INC.
1993

Clear Credit

JOHN CROWE IS responsible for much of the material regarding automobiles, aircraft, and for the extensive treatment of firearms; Kenneth Faig, Jr., supplied valuable information about public records; Justin Hynes additional newspapers and press agencies; Andrew Leman for currency of the times and many other efforts not apparent; Paul McConnel for notes about everyday equipment and newspaper clippings; Anne Merritt for clothing styles of the 1920s; Kevin Ross for profiles of Andrews, Byrd, Cayce, Edison, Fort, Goddard, Houdini, and Tesla; Lucya Szachnowski for info about public records, Lloyd's, Interpol, and nearly all the museum and library write-ups. All other material is by Keith Herber.

Special thanks go to John Crowe for patience with long phone calls, J. Todd Kingrea for uncredited suggestions and thoughts, Andrew Leman for numerous intangibles, Gregory Detwiler whose efforts are yet to see the light of day and has more reason to be upset than anybody—and to all others who contributed in some small way but whose names do not appear here. Thanks to all.

— Keith Herber

Introduction

TOO OFTEN 1920s investigators find themselves not only baffled by the mysteries of the Cthulhu Mythos, but baffled as well by day-to-day life in America in the Roaring Twenties. Although only seventy years ago, the differences in lifestyle, technology, and human perception are all markedly different. Investigator's Companions are intended to fill this void, providing intrepid investigators with information and facts about the everyday world they live in. Rather than being forced to ask your keeper for information about your world, you may now turn to the Investigator's Companion.

Filled with facts about the world, you can learn what research facilities are available, what sorts of equipment is on the market, and who might one talk with to learn more about some particular mystery. Use this book to challenge your keeper. Write a letter to explorer Roy Chapman Andrews asking about a strange artifact you've found, or contact Kentucky mystic Edgar Cayce and ask for a reading. See what sort of reply your keeper provides

Aside from a few new skills, this book also provides an extensive treatment of firearms common to the era. In an effort to expand the range of available weaponry some adjustments to the original CoC rules were necessary. This includes alterations to rates of fire, base ranges, and other factors. Although these, and other variants, are recommended for adoption, it is up to the keeper whether or not to accept these changes. His is the final word.

Future books planned for this series include a volume of 1920s Investigator Occupations, and a handbook for Gaslight investigators. Keeper's Compendiums will deal strictly with the Mythos and related topics.

Complete

Contents

PART-1

The Roaring Twenties

A time of Prosperity, Social Unrest,
Prohibition and Gangsterism,
Chronology of the Roaring Twenties.

SOME CALLED IT THE JAZZ AGE, others the Plastics Age, a time of "flaming youth" dubbed "the lost generation" by Gertrude Stein. F. Scott Fitzgerald wrote of Great Gatsby, Henry Ford fulfilled his dream of a working man's automobile, Josephine Baker shocked audiences on two sides of the Atlantic, the Marx Brothers and Mae West wowed them on Broadway, and rum-running gangsters and bootleggers like Al Capone and Dutch Schultz shot it out with J. Edgar Hoover and Eliot Ness. President Warren G. Harding's "normalcy" gave way to "Coolidge prosperity," the stock market climbed, and everyone dreamed of becoming a millionaire.

Women's suffrage was gained in 1920, but the symbol of the times was the 'flapper,' a young woman who seemed more interested in personal freedom than political activism. A shock to pre-war morals, flappers discarded brassieres and corsets in favor of lightweight dresses, bobbed hair, rolled-down stockings, and cigarettes. Sometimes called 'jazz babies' the flapper was a symbol of the era—the party girl who wore lipstick and rouge, and rode in a rumble seat sharing a hip flask—a 'sheba' to her boyfriend's 'sheik.'

Black and white America found some common ground with the latter's discovery of the Cotton Club in New York's Harlem; Louis Armstrong and Bessie Smith become actual recording stars. The tango craze of the 'teens gave way to such dances as the Charleston, the Shimmy, and the Black Bottom, all, along with flappers in general, condemned by conservative elements of society. Fads like Mah-Jong flourished briefly, only to give way to Crossword puzzles, or flagpole sitting, or dance marathons. Ex-military and mail pilots toured the country stunting in Jennys, selling rides in their open cockpit flying machines to nervous first-time aeronauts. Hollywood began cranking out films by the hundreds, making stars of Buster Keaton, Lillian Gish, Douglas Fairbanks, Charlie Chaplin, and Clara Bow.

The rise of the automobile brought an unprecedented freedom to a young America. With over 23 million vehicles registered by the end of the decade, the U.S. government embarked upon the greatest highway building program in history, criss-crossing the continent with a net-

drink~ Flapper

A Snappy Drink

Union Bottling Works
Beaumont Texas

work of poured concrete roads. And the booming growth of radio ushers in a new era of communication—and mass media.

Dial telephones are all the rage, eliminating the need to contact an operator. New electric appliances appear everyday including washing machines, toasters, curling irons and corn poppers—even blow dryers for the hair. Houses are not yet wired for outlets. Most appliances have screw-in plugs that fit the standard light-bulb socket, but this is changing fast and new electric 'refrigerators' are fast replacing the venerable ice box.

There are a couple economic depressions, one in 1921, and a smaller one in 1924, but in general it is, for America, a decade of unprecedented growth and prosperity.

A Time of Prosperity

While the postwar years take a heavy toll in Europe, the United States emerges the healthiest and strongest nation in the world. Nearly untouched by the ravages of the War, it has benefited greatly by wartime mobilization of industry and government-regulated growth and expansion.

New York City is now the financial capital of the world, its Stock Exchange the heart of American investment. In 1920 a seat on the Exchange sells for $60,000. By 1929 the price has soared to a half million dollars or more. Millionaires abound, names like Mellon, Rockefeller, and DuPont are known round the world, and men like Henry Ford are living proof that—with a little effort—even the commonest man can rise to great heights. By the end of the decade it seems that everybody has an investment, from housewife to chauffeur.

Real Estate speculation reached a new peak in 1925 with the Florida land boom. Recently subdivided lots doubled, tripled, and quintupled in a matter of months while flocks of northerners, driving their automobiles down the Dixie Highway, descended on the sleepy state hoping to purchase the retirement home of their dreams. Miami grows from a sleepy village of 5,741 in 1910 to a bustling city of nearly 160,000 by the end of the decade. The buying mania probably reached its peak when one developer hired famed New England orator William Jennings Bryan to sit on a raft in a Florida lagoon and publicly extol the virtues of the Florida climate. The dream started to unravel in early 1926 when the whole scheme of non-binding purchases began to crumble. Investors who had cursed themselves for once selling a lot for $12 only to watch the price rise to a $100 or more, were shocked to find the same property suddenly reverted back to them through a whole chain of speculators who had purchased on non-binding agreements. Not only did this investor never receive his original $12, he often found he sometimes owed tax bills and other charges made against the now nearly worthless property. Florida's 'Gold Coast' was hit by a killer hurricane in late 1926, putting the final nail in the coffin of Florida's land boom.

But growth and development were happening everywhere and the city skyscraper became a symbol of the times. A truly American architectural form, the low city skylines of the early century gave way to the spires and towers of capitalism rising everywhere from New York, to Detroit, to Chicago, while architects, investors, and even city fathers vied for the honor of building the tallest structure. It reached a peak when ground was broken for New York City's Empire State Building. Soaring 102 stories and 1250 feet into the air, it is for decades unchallenged as the tallest building in the world, and the symbol of an era. Before its doors are opened in 1931 people are already selling apples in the street.

Social Unrest

Not everyone believed in the dream and many felt shut out of the game—or disagreed with it. Factory and foundry workers, coal miners and street car operators, police and telephone operators, all at one time or another found wages inadequate in the face of rising inflation. Industrialists and owners conspired to keep wages down, and

unions appeared among the ranks. The International Workers of the World—the 'Wobblies'—called for "One Big Union." But to the minds of many, unions were associated with anarchists, socialists, and foreign influence-peddlers. In Russia the new bolshevik leaders have called for a "world revolution of workers," and to many labor unions equate with Communists and violent, revolutionary overthrow of the government. In response, Attorney General A. Mitchell Palmer, the "Fighting Quaker," orders raids on the headquarters of various socialist and communist organizations, arresting their ringleaders and deporting many to Russia.

Songs of the 20s

1920: "I'll Be With You in Apple Blossom Time," Jerome Kern's "Look for the Silver Lining," "When My Baby Smiles at Me."

1921: "Sheik of Araby," "I'm Just Wild About Harry," "Ain't We Got Fun."

1922: "Chicago (That Toddlin' Town)," "Toot, Toot, Tootsie Goodbye," "Way Down Yonder in New Orleans," "I Wish I Could Shimmy Like Sister Kate," "Carolina in the Morning."

1923: "Yes! We Have No Bananas!", "Who's Sorry Now?", "That Old Gang of Mine," Bessie Smith records "Down-Hearted Blues" for Columbia Records.

1924: "Indian Love Call," Gershwin's "Fascinatin' Rhythm," "It Had To Be You," " Tea for Two," "California Here I Come."

1925: "I'm Sittin' On Top of the World," "Alabamy Bound," "If You Knew Susie Like I Know Susie," "Sweet Georgia Brown," "Yes Sir, That's My Baby," Fats Waller's "Squeeze Me."

1926: "Are You Lonesome Tonight," "Bye, Bye, Blackbird," "When the Red, Red Robin Comes Bob, Bob, Bobbin' Along," "Tip Toe Through the Tulips."

1927: "Lucky Lindy," "My Blue Heaven," "Swonderful," "Side by Side," "Ain't She Sweet," "Me and My Shadow."

1928: "I Can't Give You Anything But Love," "You're the Cream in My Coffee," "Makin' Whoopee." "I Wanna Be Loved by You" eventually gives birth to the Betty Boop character.

1929: "Puttin' On the Ritz," "Ain't Misbehavin'," "Star Dust," "Singin' in the Rain," "With a Song in My Heart," "Those Wedding Bells are Breaking Up that Old Gang of Mine."

1930: "I Got Rhythm," "Embraceable You," "Sunny Side of the Street.'

The early decade sees numerous strikes, mob violence, and even murder. Anarchists send bombs through the U.S. mails and Mayday paraders are viciously attacked in the streets by gangs of 'patriots.' In 1920 foreign-born Sacco and Vanzetti are arrested for the robbery of an armored car and the murder of the guards. After lengthy trials and appeals, and much national and international publicity and protest, the pair are finally executed on August 22, 1927.

Books of the 20s

1920: Agatha Christie publishes her first Hercule Poirot novel *The Mysterious Affair at Styles*, *The Man of the Forest* by Zane Grey, *This Side of Paradise* by F. Scott Fitzgerald.

1921: H.G. Well's *Outline of History*, *Mainstreet* by Sinclair Lewis, *The Mysterious Rider* by Zane Grey, *The Age of Innocence* by Edith Wharton, *The Sheik* by Edith Hull.

1922: Sinclair Lewis writes *Babbitt*, *Diet and Health* introduces calorie counting and remains a best seller for five years, *The Story of Mankind* by Van Loof, *Showboat* by Edna Ferber, *The Outline of Science* by J. Arthur Thomson, *Ulysses* by James Joyce.

1923: Emile Coué's *Self-Mastery Through Conscious Auto-Suggestion* prompts a mental health and self-improvement fad. *Etiquette: The Blue Book of Social Usage* by Emily Post.

1924: *Call of the Canyon* by Zane Grey.

1925: Sinclair Lewis's *Arrowsmith*, F. Scott Fitzgerald's *The Great Gatsby*, Virginia Woolf's *Mrs. Dalloway*, Theodore Dreiser's *An American Tragedy*, Charlie Chan debuts in Earl Bigger's *House Without a Key*.

1926: Agatha Christie achieves fame with *The Murder of Roger Ackroyd*, Will Durant's *The Story of Philosophy* sells two million copies, Ernest Hemingway writes *The Sun Also Rises*, and Anita Loos *Gentlemen Prefer Blondes*.

1927: Sinclair Lewis publishes *Elmer Gantry*, Virginia Woolf, *To the Lighthouse*.

1928: *Point Counter Point* by Aldous Huxley, D.H. Lawrence's *Lady Chatterley's Lover* is widely banned, *The Bridge of San Luis Rey* by Thorton Wilder goes on to win a Pulitzer.

1929: Herman Hesse's *Steppenwolf* (1927) appears in English translation, Sinclair Lewis's *Dodsworth*, Hemingway's *A Farewell to Arms*, Thomas Wolfe writes *Look Homeward Angel*, Erich Maria Remarque recalls the Great War in *All Quiet on the Western Front*, Henry Faulkner's *The Sound and the Fury*, Dashiell Hammett's *The Dain Curse*, and Robert Ripley's *Believe It, or Not!*.

The Ku Klux Klan

Intolerance is everywhere on the rise. The Ku Klux Klan reemerged on the American scene in 1915, inspired by D.W. Griffith's classic film *Birth of a Nation*. Small at first, in 1920 the KKK hits on the idea of selling memberships, a portion of the fee being kicked back to the salesman and those above him in a classic 'pyramid scheme.' By 1924 the Klan's numbers are estimated at 4,500,000 and public marches are held in Washington D.C. and other cities. Garbed in white robes, their identities hidden by tall, peaked hats, the Klan vilifies blacks, Jews, and Catholics, and are accused of a number of violent assaults and murders.

Prohibition and Gangsterism

It was also a time when, in an unprecedented move, the country went 'dry.' Using a war-time statute, the drinking of alcohol was prohibited by the 18th amendment to the Constitution—the first ever to restrict a freedom. Although referendums in such places as Chicago showed the ban opposed by as many as three to one, Congress posed little opposition when the measure was introduced. Before long the amendment had been ratified by the minimum two-thirds of the states. The Volstead act, imposed in the summer of 1919, put teeth in Prohibition, allowing for the arrest and prosecution of those who violated the law.

But Prohibition had little effect on the great many people who wished to continue drinking. The U.S.'s thousands of miles of international borders are impossible to guard and liquor flowed in from Canada, the Caribbean, and Mexico, while small 'alky cookers' and illegal stills fired up all over the country. Most big cities, particularly in the north and east, did little to check the flow of illegal alcohol—most of the members of government and police preferring to either ignore, or actively participate in the unlawful production and distribution. Speakeasies, supposedly secret places where patrons could drink, were more often quite well-known. The most famous in New

York was undoubtedly "Jack and Charlie's" at 21 W. 52nd Street, known then and now as '21.' In 1925 *Variety*, the entertainment magazine, estimates that Harlem alone has eleven high-class, white-trade night clubs, and at least five hundred lesser, low-down speakeasies.

Supplying illegal alcohol to a thirsty citizenry was big business and the 1920s saw the rise of gangsterism in America. Previously little more than hoods and muggers running small, local protection rackets, the burgeoning black market in alcohol provided the opportunity for huge profits. Using their ill-gotten gains to buy protection from police and judges, rum-running was estimated to be a two billion dollar a year industry employing some half-million workers. Competition was fierce, and gangland killings spread across the nation from city to city, various small time hoods fighting for control of local business. In New York, Dutch Schultz and Legs Diamond war with Myer Lansky and Lucky Luciano, while the Purple Gang runs Detroit, and Cleveland, Philadelphia, Boston, and Baltimore all come under control of well-financed and increasingly organized gangsters. But it is in Chicago where the problem is most evident.

Al Capone

Alphonse Capone arrived in Chicago in 1920. Formerly a thug with New York City's vicious Five Points gang, Capone was invited to Chicago by his old friend Johnny Torrio. Capone proves a worthy lieutenant, forming an alliance with the Sicilian Genna brothers, and working out a truce with the North Side gang led by Irishman Dion O'Banion. The truce proves a shaky one, and in 1925 O'Banion is assassinated in his flower shop by unknown gunmen. War soon breaks out as Hymie Weiss, taking over for O'Banion, attacks Johnny Torrio in front of his home, almost killing him. Three of the six Genna brothers meet death within the next few months before Weiss is finally gunned down in the streets. Capone, following the retirement of a suddenly fearful Torrio, takes over. The gang wars reach a peak on St. Valentine's Day, 1929, when eight members of the North Side gang, now led by George 'Bugs' Moran, are lined up against a garage wall and executed. Public affection for gangsters wanes as the wars escalate and innocent citizens are more and more often caught in the cross-fire. Near the end of the decade the federal govern-

ment takes steps to shut down the mobs, sending men like Eliot Ness to clean up places like Chicago. Prohibition is finally repealed in 1933, but not before organized crime has gotten a solid foothold that is never lost.

Government Corruption

Government corruption was rampant as well. The untimely death of President Warren G. Harding in 1923 (sometimes rumored to have been the result of poison administered by his jealous wife) led to the discovery of a nest of embezzlement and trust violations that was to become known as the Teapot Dome Scandal. Diligent investigators also turn up irregularities in the Veteran's Bureau, the Alien Property Custody Department, and discover dozens of graft schemes related to Prohibition.

Broadway Stage of the 20s

1920: *The Ziegfield Follies* stars Fanny Brice in *Rose of Washington Square*.

1921: Sardi's restaurant opens in the theatre district of Manhattan. Fanny Brice follows up last year's hit with *Second Hand Rose*.

1922: Sam Harris produces *Rain*.

1923: Josephine Baker stars in *Shuffle Along*, a Harlem review brought to Broadway. David Belasco produces *Laugh, Clown, Laugh*.

1924: Noel Coward's *The Vortex*, The Marx Brothers appear in *I'll Say She Is*, black actor Paul Robeson stars in Eugene O'Neill's *Emperor Jones*, Josephine Baker appears in *Chocolate Dandies*, then leaves America for Paris.

1925: Noel Coward writes *Hay Fever*, Sam Harris produces *The Jazz Singer* featuring George Jessel, The Marx Brothers star in *The Cocoanuts*.

1926: Mae West shocks them with *Sex*, David Belasco produces *Lu Lu Belle*.

1927: *Showboat* begins a record breaking run of over 500 performances. Broadway hits its peak with 268 opening nights this year.

1928: Newspaperman Ben Hecht hits it big with *The Front Page*, the Marx Brothers' star in *Animal Crackers*, Mae West appears in *Diamond Lil*, Bert Lahr in *Hold Everything*.

1929: Noel Coward writes the musical *Bittersweet*, Billie Burke appears in *Happy Husbands*.

1930: Ethel Merman stars in Gershwin's *Girl Crazy*, Fanny Brice in *Sweet and Low*.

1920s Currency

THERE ARE SOME notable differences in the currency of the 1920s. Paper money is larger, approximately a half-inch longer and wider. Denominations include $1, $2, $5, $10, $20, $50, $100, $500, $1000, $5000, and $10,000. Many were actual gold and silver certificates, not mere Federal Reserve Notes.

Coinage includes the one-cent copper Lincoln penny, the five-cent buffalo nickel, the silver ten-cent Liberty dime, silver twenty-five cent Liberty quarter, and Liberty half-dollars and 'silver dollars.' Gold coins in circulation are: the gold quarter-eagle, the half-eagle, eagle, and double-eagle, worth $2.50, $5.00, $10.00, and $20.00 respectively.

Various investigations, hearings, and trials continue throughout the decade.

Popular Diversions

When not reading of the exploits of gangsters and corrupt politicians in the tabloids or of Clarence Darrow's efforts to defend evolution in Tennessee, they indulge in the exploits and excesses of their favorite movie stars, chronicled in *Variety* and *True Screen*. Movies are enormously successful, particularly after 'talkies' become popular in 1927. The lives of film celebrities are followed in minute detail by fans everywhere. Spurred by the Hollywood industry, thousands flock to California and the population of Los Angeles soars from 319,000 in 1910, to over a 1,336,000 by the end of the 20s.

The home phonograph grows in popularity. Still driven by hand-cranked springs, high-quality models boasting superior reproduction cost $150 and more. Sales of records reach the millions by the middle of the decade, honor and fame being heaped on the songwriters rather than the performers. As radio gains in popularity, record sales take a drastic plunge.

Sports

Sporting events take on a new popularity and stadiums capable of holding fifty to seventy thousand people and more are routinely built. Babe Ruth stuns baseball when he hits 59 home runs in 1921 and 60 in 1927. Footballer Red Grange quits college to turn professional and before the end of the year is invited to the White House to meet the president. Jack Dempsey is the best-known heavyweight of the decade and it is estimated that forty million people listen to the radio broadcast of his unsuccessful bid to regain the title from Tunney in 1927. Losing the crown on a disputed count, five radio listeners were reported to have died of heart attacks. Golf is a sport both

followed and played by millions, and tennis courts—and tennis fashions—spring up all over the country.

The Automobile

But automobile touring is undoubtedly the fastest growing pastime. Henry Ford's affordable automobile and an ever-growing network of highways have provided a new freedom for the youth of the country. The average American can now load up his automobile and drive off for a week or more at a time, visiting and touring the country at his leisure, and at far less expense than train travel and hotels. An entire highway industry of garages, filling stations, diners, chicken shacks, and auto camps has sprung up to fill the demands of the new generation of motorists, forever changing the face of America. Tents and camping gear are available allowing the motorist to sleep by the road, avoiding the expense of hotels and restaurants. By the end of the decade over fifteen million vehicles a year are visiting various national parks and forests. Centered in Detroit, the booming business in automobiles has given rise to a new breed of millionaires named Ford and Chrysler.

October, 1929

The end came in October, 1929, when the bottom fell out of the stock market. Many predicted a rebound, but it was soon shown otherwise. Millionaires were wiped out, some committing suicide rather than face the prospect of an impotent future. Workers were laid off by the millions, and unrest spread among those still employed. Economic depression grips the world and Charles Lindbergh, the "Lone Eagle," everybody's hero, loses his young son to kidnap and murder. It somehow signifies the end of an era.

The 1920s Wardrobe

ALTHOUGH CLOTHING FADS are many, ranging from raccoon coats to bell-bottom pants to flapper's dresses, the majority of Americans dress more conservatively. Business meetings and other professional engagements are no place for 'elephant' pants with huge, 30-inch cuffs. Such are for the young, not the professional.

While dramatically more casual than prior times, formalities are still observed. Both sexes wear hats and gloves when leaving the house to shop or attend church. Cloth handkerchiefs are carried, and shirts are starched and ironed. Only laborers and cowhands wear denim jeans. The rules of appropriate dress are known to all well-bred people and as the middle class increases its spending power, it is increasingly difficult to distinguish class simply by clothing.

Men's Styles

The most dramatic change in men's clothing occurred around the turn of the century when the modern business suit was adopted as standard attire for the working professional. A properly dressed man wears a dark suit, white shirt, tie, dark shoes and socks. Pants are held up with suspenders, the points of shirt collars held down by a pin. Walking sticks are not yet uncommon and a true gentleman always wears a hat and gloves. Evening attire may be informal: a tuxedo with unstarched shirt and cummerbund or cotton pique vest, or fully formal with tails, starched shirt, and vest.

Inspired by the growing interest in sports, men's clothing of the 20s is loosely fitted, providing ease of movement. Undershirts and shorts are fast replacing the old union suit, and wristwatches are now more common than chains and fobs. Short hair and clean-shaven faces are the rule—even a small mustache is noteworthy.

Men's shirts still have detachable collars and cuffs although 1920s collars are soft compared to their stiff predecessors of earlier times. It is well into the next decade before the inclusion of rayon makes fabrics durable enough that collars and cuffs no longer need be periodically replaced.

This decade sees the introduction of lighter colors and fabrics in men's clothing and warm weather clothing grows popular: the white linen dinner jacket, white flannel trousers, Panama hat or straw boater are now perfectly acceptable at many occasions.

Coat and Hat

Coats are worn long and loose. The popular raccoon coat, introduced for driving and attending winter football games, is later replaced by less bulky, deep pile camel hair coats.

Films of the 20s

1919: Theda Bara, the 'Vamp,' stars in *Salome*. D.W. Griffith directs *Broken Blossoms*.

1920: Lon Chaney stars in *The Penalty*, Lillian Gish in *Orphans of the Storm*, John Barrymore in *Dr. Jekyll and Mr. Hyde*, Mary Pickford in *Pollyana*, and Douglas Fairbanks (Sr.) in *The Mark of Zorro*. United Artists film company is formed by Charlie Chaplin, Mary Pickford, Doug Fairbanks, and legendary producer and director D.W. Griffith.

1921: Rudolph Valentino becomes an overnight sensation with *The Sheik* and *The Four Horsemen of the Apocalypse*. Mack Sennett makes *A Small Town Idol*, Charlie Chaplin stars in *The Kid*, Douglas Fairbanks in *The Three Musketeers*.

1922: Henry Hull and Carol Dempster co-star in *One Exciting Night*, Douglas Fairbanks in *Robin Hood*, and F.W. Murnau directs *Nosferatu* in Germany. *Nanook of the North* by American explorer Robert Flaherty defines the film documentary.

1923: Lon Chaney stars in *The Hunchback of Notre Dame*, Cecil B. DeMille produces *The Ten Commandments*, William S. Hart stars in *Wild Bill Hickok*, comedian Harold Lloyd wows them in *Safety Last*, comedy director Mack Sennett produces the spoof, *The Shriek of Araby*.

1924: Harold Lloyd in *Girl Shy*, Buster Keaton in *The Navigator*, Douglas Fairbanks in *The Thief of Baghdad*, John Ford directs *The Iron Horse*.

1925: Lon Chaney stars in *The Phantom of the Opera*, William S. Hart in *Tumbleweeds*, Harold Lloyd in *The Freshman*, Adolphe Menjou in *The Sorrows of Satan*, Buster Keaton in *Seven Chances*, Charlie Chaplin in *The Gold Rush*, and Willis O'brien brings prehistoric creatures to life in *The Lost World*.

1926: Joan Crawford debuts in *Pretty Ladies*, Greta Garbo stars in *The Torrent*, Fritz Lang directs the classic *Metropolis*, John Barrymore stars in first non-musical talkie, *Don Juan*, Buster Keaton in *The General*, Francis X. Bushman stars in Ben-Hur. Valentino's funeral touches off a mob hysteria in Manhattan that leaves the funeral parlor looted by souvenir seekers.

1927: Lon Chaney in *London After Midnight*, Cecil B. DeMille produces *King of Kings*, Great Garbo in *Flesh and the Devil* and, with John Gilbert, in *Love*, Al Jolson stars in the first full-length talking picture *The Jazz Singer*, William Fox introduces *Movietone Newsreels*, and Clara Bow becomes the 'It' girl—the quintessential flapper—when she stars in *It*.

1928: Joan Crawford stars in *Our Dancing Daughters*, Charlie Chaplin in *The Circus*, Victor McGlaglen in *A Girl in Every Port*, Mickey Mouse in *Steamboat Willie*, Clara Bow in *Red Hair, Three Weekends,* and *The Fleet's In*, Howard Hughes produces *Two Arabian Nights*.

1929: Gary Cooper stars in *The Virginian*, Greta Garbo in *Wild Orchids*, The Marx Brothers in *The Cocoanuts*, Ronald Coleman in *Bulldog Drummond*, Douglas Fairbanks in *The Man in the Iron Mask*, Lionel Barrymore in *Mysterious Island*, and Alfred Hitchcock directs *Blackmail*.

1930: Greta Garbo stars in Eugene O'neill's *Anna Christie*, the Marx Brothers in *Animal Crackers*, Josef Sternberg directs Marlene Dietrich in *The Blue Angel*, Howard Hughes produces *Hell's Angels*, Walter Huston plays *Abraham Lincoln* while John Barrymore portrays Ahab in *Moby Dick*.

Sports of the 20s

Baseball: Judge Kenesaw Mountain Landis is named the first Commissioner of Baseball (1920) in the wake of the infamous World Series betting scandal. The undisputed star of the decade is Babe Ruth who's salary at one time exceeds that of the President of the United States (Ruth "had a better year"). Other favorites are Ty Cobb, Rogers Hornsby, Branch Rickey, George Sisler, and Grover Cleveland Alexander. Baseball also features such colorful managers as John McGraw of the N.Y. Giants and Connie Mack of the Philadelphia Athletics.

Basketball: Familiar teams exist like the Boston Celtics and New York Knickerbockers, but few remember the Cleveland Rosenblums. Joseph Lapchick, a center, is the biggest star. (By the way, the baskets still have bottoms in them.)

Boxing: Professional boxing grows in popularity and legitimacy. Jack Dempsey rules as Heavyweight Champ for the first part of the decade, but loses the title to Gene Tunney in 1926. In 1927 American sportswriter Paul Gallico organizes the first amateur Golden Gloves contest.

Football: College football is more closely followed than the pro game but that changes when college star Red Grange drops out of school in his senior year to play with first the Chicago Bears and then the New York Giants. Well-known college coaches include Notre Dame's Knute Rockne, Pop Warner who in 1924 leaves the University of Pennsylvania to coach at California's Stanford University, and John Heisman of Pennsylvania and Rice.

Golf: Walter Hagen, Gene Sarazen, and Chick Evans are the best known professional golfers of the decade, but rising youngster Bobby Jones poses a threat.

Polo: Ex-flying ace Tommy Hitchcock, Jr., dominates the polo fields and is widely considered the best player of all time.

Tennis: The most popular tennis celebrity is Bill Tilden but the Frenchmen Jacques Brugnon captures the Davis Cup 1927-32.

During the day a felt hat or a derby is worn with a suit; a soft cap is sufficient for attending sporting events. Top hats usually accompany formal evening wear.

Women's Fashions

Women's fashions have undergone the most dramatic change. The brassiere has replaced the corset and the 'natural' silhouette has become fashionable. Long-waisted dresses with short skirts—and even shorter hair—are in dramatic contrast to prior decades where women stood stiffly erect with long hair piled high, rigid collars, cinched waists, hems inches from the floor, and ankles protected by boots. Today's woman moves at too fast a pace to let her clothes slow her down.

The World War provided many women with the opportunity to work outside the home for the first time and they were quick to discover that their high collars, full sleeves, and corsets were an impediment, and long hair that tumbled into machinery a distinct danger. After the War many women went back to their homes, but few returned to the corset.

Current Styles

The biggest revolution is in lingerie. The corset is replaced with brassiere and panties, or chemise and knickers of *crepe de chine* or silk jersey. At first simple, unadorned garments, they are soon enhanced with lace, embroidery, and applique. Slips of the same materials are worn as required. One newspaper report claims the typical working girl spends almost 40% of her earnings on underwear.

The current fashion silhouette features a lithe, long-waisted look. Hemlines through the decade first move up to the bottom of the knee, then down to the ankle, then back to the knee. By 1930 the mid-calf length is established, remaining the favored daytime length until World War II. High hemlines are particularly popular with flappers, though much of society views them as little less than scandalous. But women of all classes have adopted new freedoms: smoking and drinking in public, wearing make-up, exposing bare arms after dark, and clipping their hair short.

Bobbed and the shingle hairstyles are the rage. Bobby pins are introduced to keep hair from falling into one's eyes, or to achieve the desired curl on the forehead. For those who keep their hair long the popular hair-do is the chignon, or bun at the back of the head. Makeup, previously scorned by all but prostitutes and actresses, is now popular with ladies of all social classes.

Hats and Accessories

Of the several types of popular hats, the tight fitting, undecorated felt cloche covering the entire head is the signature design of the era. Introduced by the French designer Reboux, its popularity quickly eclipses the beret, the big chapeau, and the tricorn.

A larger hand bag is needed to carry cosmetic cases and cigarettes and is added to the daytime ensemble of dress, coat, hat and gloves. Pumps have replaced boots, and feature a variety of straps, buckles and heels.

Evening Wear

Daytime clothing is usually dark and muted but evening styles sparkle. Not only are hemlines leaping to the knee,

necklines plunge front and back, and arms are left bare. Trains from the hip, or other ornament, are common fashion. Front hems often remain at the knee while back hems dip low to the floor. Evening colors offer an array of pinks, reds, yellows, oranges and purples, and the all-white ensemble is introduced. At the beginning of the decade, velvets, crepe, and lace are common, with new synthetics—especially velvets—becoming popular later. Ornaments of fringe, tassels, or beaded embroidery are favorites. The long pearl necklace is popular in the evening, along with turbans of gold or silver.

Sports Wear

"Ease of movement," "Casual attire for the fast pace of modern life," "Sports ensemble," are phrases ringing from the pages of the fashion magazines. The growing popularity of sports has contributed to many clothing innovations. Aside from the replacement of the union suit by sleeveless undershirts and shorts, the less restrictive leather belt is gaining favor over suspenders, and soft caps are favored when golfing or bicycling. Indoors, men find the house robe or lounging jacket comfortable and it is here that the masculine taste for colorful fabrics finds expression. Bright striped robes and blazers are quite acceptable at the beach or pool as well. The V-neck sweater and the cotton knit shirt with open collar are introduced, manufactured by Danton and La Coste. Knickers become so popular with the young that they stay fashionable for men well into their thirties.

For women, sleeveless sweaters are suitable for tennis and golf, jodhpurs for riding, and ski pants when trekking through the snow. A short string of pearls sets off most daytime wear. Lounging pajamas are popular with the upper classes. Consisting of a tunic over loose pants, they usually feature bands of contrasting color at the hemlines. Light green pajamas with purple bands would be typical. Hollywood films of the 1930s make these outfits famous. The beach is the only place a woman shows more skin than she does in the evening. The one-piece maillot bathing suit is fast replacing the bulky swim wear of the past. ∎

Chronology of the Roaring Twenties

1918: November 11, Armistice signed and the War ends.

1919: April 28, the first in a series of mail bombs are discovered. Sent to government officials and industrialists, they spark the first post-war Red Scare riots. **June 26,** America's first tabloid newspaper, the New York *Daily News*, appears. *True Stories* magazine is launched, taking advantage of the market for sex and scandal magazines. **July 1,** the War-time Prohibition Act takes effect. Summer race riots rock Chicago for days after the drowning of a black youth who ventured to near the 'white' beach. **September 9,** the Boston police strike results in riots, and is followed by national steel and coal strikes. **November 19,** Congress rejects Wilson's League of Nations. The Volstead Act is passed, allowing for legal enforcement of the Prohibition amendment. The ZR-3 dirigible (later named the R-34 *Los Angeles*) makes the first airship crossing of the Atlantic from England to Long Island, piloted by famed German airship pilot, Hugo Eckener. New York gambler Arnold Rothstein fixes baseball's World Series, paying members of the Chicago White Sox to throw the championship. By year's end an estimated one to two million American workers are on strike. Government raids, organized by 24-year-old J. Edgar Hoover, net hundreds of suspected communists; many are deported to Russia.

News travels fast in the 1920s.

1920: August 8, Woman's Suffrage. **September 16,** a bomb rocks Wall Street in New York, killing forty people outright. **November 3,** KDKA radio in Pittsburgh broadcasts the returns of the Harding-Cox presidential election; Harding defeats Cox and takes office the following spring. Babe Ruth takes the batting title from Ty Cobb. The Ku Klux Klan, revived in 1915, begins selling memberships across the country, swelling its ranks. Man o' War is the race horse of the year, and probably the decade. Eskimo Pie ice cream bars are introduced. In the wake of the World Series betting scandal, Judge Kenesaw Mountain Landis is named the first Baseball Commissioner. Sacco and Vanzetti are accused of robbing an armor car and murdering the guards. Al Capone comes to Chicago from New York at the invitation of gangster Johnny Torrio.

1921: July 2, peace is signed with Germany. The first Miss America 'bathing beauty' contest is held in Atlantic City, New Jersey. Lionel sells its one millionth electric train set. White people 'discover' Harlem and the famous Cotton Club. Sardi's restaurant opens in New York's theatre district. Jack Dempsey defeats the Frenchmen Carpentier to retain the heavyweight boxing title. Babe Ruth hits fifty-nine home runs. Film star Fatty Arbuckle's career is ruined by a scandal involving the death of a young actress in San Francisco's St. Francis Hotel.

1922: February 22, President Harding has a radio installed in his office. September 16, the Halls-Mill homicide case involving a minister and his married choir leader is called "the murder of the decade" by the tabloids. By September Mah-Jong sets are being imported by the thousands; some cost as much as $500. Radio sales top $60 million. The treasures of King Tut's tomb are revealed to the world, sparking an interest in Egyptian art and style that lasts the rest of the decade.

1923: August 2, Warren G. Harding dies in office, Vice-president Calvin Coolidge takes over. The Charleston dance craze, condemned by many as immoral, sweeps the nation. H.L. Mencken's *American Mercury* magazine makes its first appearance near the end of the year. Dance marathons become popular, followed by rocking-chair marathons and talking marathons called "Verb-and-Noun Derbies."

1924: Simon & Schuster publish their first Crossword puzzle book, setting off a nationwide craze. Turtleneck sweaters are popularized by playwright Noel Coward. Gershwin's *Rhapsody in Blue* premieres at New York's Aeolian theatre to mixed reviews. Membership in the Ku Klux Klan reaches a peak with an estimated 4.5 million members. Young Leopold and Loeb, accused of brutally murdering fourteen-year-old Bobby Franks, are defended by Clarence Darrow. *Time* magazine honors Leo Bakeland, the inventor of Bakelite and, citing the recent inventions of cellophane, vinyl, and others, titles the era "The Plastic Age." Alvin 'Shipwreck' Kelly starts a flagpole sitting craze. Clarence Birdseye founds General Seafoods, Inc., and perfects his fast-freezing process. International Business Machines (IBM) is founded.

1925: The Scopes Monkey Trial in Dayton, Tennessee, pits Clarence Darrow and evolution against William Jennings Bryan and creationism. Darrow loses the case, but his defense is generally viewed as a victory for science and evolution. The exhausted Bryan dies a few days later. The plight of Kentuckian Floyd Collins, trapped in a cave, is carefully followed by millions of newspaper readers and radio listeners across the country. An early instance of mass media interest, the hapless Collins dies on the eighteenth day. The U.S. Navy dirigible *Shenandoah* is wrecked, and all aboard killed. The Florida land boom reaches its peak. Golf is a half-billion dollar a year industry. Red Grange quits college in his senior year to play professional football with first the Chicago Bears, and then the New York Giants. Gene Tunney defeats Jack Dempsey in Philadelphia.

1926: Western Air Service (later TWA) begins regular passenger service. Hollywood hits a peak, producing over 750 feature films this year. Rudolph Valentino dies of a ruptured appendix, his funeral in New York City touching off a near-riot that leaves the funeral parlor looted by souvenir seekers. Contract Bridge is introduced to America and is an immediate hit. Richard Byrd successfully flies over the North Pole. California evangelist Aimee Semple McPherson 'disappears' from a beach, causing a sensation before miraculously reappearing several days later. A giant hurricane rakes Florida's Gold Coast, killing 400 people and putting an end to the Florida land boom. Hymie Weiss leads a convoy of ten cars past Al Capone's headquarters in the Hawthorne Hotel, raking the building with over a thousand rounds of automatic gunfire in a blatant, daylight drive-by shooting; Capone is uninjured.

1927: Charles Lindbergh flies solo across the Atlantic to France, returning home a national and international hero. Jolson's talkie *The Jazz Singer* grosses 3.5 million dollars at the box office, reshaping the Hollywood film industry. Records now selling in the millions. New York theatres hit an all-time peak with 268 openings covered by twenty-four daily newspapers. In August, Sacco and Vanzetti finally go to the electric chair. The Ford Model 'A' is released, replacing the old Model 'T.' Babe Ruth hits sixty home runs. Jack Dempsey loses his bid to regain the title, falling to Gene Tunney in Chicago while an estimated forty million listen in on the radio. Aimee Semple McPherson founds the Church of the Foursquare Gospel near Los Angeles. David Sarnoff founds NBC (the National Broadcasting Corporation).

1928: March 3, the Stock Market begins to rise, beginning what is called its 'sensational' phase. **June 18**, polar explorer Roald Admundsen dies in an Arctic air crash while attempting to locate the missing airship *Italia*. November, Herbert Hoover is elected president. Mickey Mouse makes his debut. Sir Alexander Fleming discovers penicillin. NBC experiments with the first television broadcasts. Johannes Geiger invents the geiger counter. The highly-touted Transcontinental Foot Race, called by some "The Bunion Derby" goes off on schedule but proves a promotional and financial bust. Lynn Willis celebrates twenty-first birthday with wild, all-night Charleston party in Oregon.

1929: Transcontinental Air Transport, "Lindbergh's line," begins offering coast-to-coast flights. Hugo Eckener pilots a dirigible around the world. **February 14**, The St. Valentine's Day Massacre in a Chicago warehouse eliminates the last of Capone's rivals. Popeye makes his first appearance in the *Thimble Theater* comic strip. Radio sales pass $850 million. **October 29**, The Great Stock Market Crash.

1930: First stewardesses hired to attend passengers on the Chicago to San Francisco run. Astronomer Clyde Tombaugh discovers Pluto.

PART-2

Research & Resources

Public Records, Newspapers, Press Associations,

Libraries and Museums of Natural History.

RESEARCH IS ESSENTIAL to any investigation. It can take the form of a public records search, a close perusal of newspaper stories, in-depth research at a large library, or even expert advice from a noted professional. Not all information is necessarily available to the general public. Persuade, Fast Talk, and bribes may be of help.

Public Records

PUBLIC RECORDS REFERS to all civic and business records, census reports, land transfers, births, deaths, adoptions, medical records and others, whether the information is open to public scrutiny or not. The U.S. lacks an official National Archives before 1934; important documents are kept in the Library of Congress. Individual states, counties, and communities are responsible for their own records.

State and Local Records

Following the World War, a uniform state-level system of vital statistics registration began to emerge, although public access to these records varies from state to state. Birth records are often more restricted than marriage and death records; adoption records are routinely sealed, changed, or destroyed. Divorce records are maintained most often at the county, rather than the state, level. Civic records prior to the late 18th century are sketchy at best. Parish registers at old churches, historical societies, or genealogical societies are the best bet when looking for pre-Revolutionary War records.

Electoral registers are usually kept in local libraries and provide up-to-date information, as do city directories that list residents by name, address, and occupation. Telephone books are also helpful, but not everyone has a phone.

Property transfers, building permits, and other transactions involving real estate are always a matter of public record and available upon demand. Tracing the ownership of a particular piece of land is merely a matter of tracing the deed as it changes hands (provided the records are complete). Descriptions of the property at the time it changed hands provides clues to new construction, demolished structures, what the property may have been used for, etc. Also available to the public are local draft board records, property assessment and tax bills, building permits, applications for business licenses, and the actual financial records of the community itself.

Genealogical Societies

Interest in family lines has long been evident in the U.S. Most states have their own, privately-formed societies, and numerous smaller societies that specialize in just a few surnames. Some of the most complete include the New England Historical Genealogical Society in Massachusetts, and the Augustan Society of California. Perhaps the largest collection of genealogical records in the world is found in Salt Lake City, Utah, where the Mormons have for years been accumulating genealogical data. Most genealogical societies are open to the public.

National Records

The U.S. has conducted a national census every ten years since 1790. Census records do not become public until seventy-two years after their compilation. The first censuses recorded little more than the surname of each head of household, and the number of household members listed by sex and age group. By 1850 the census included the names, ages, birthplaces, occupation, and value of real estate for all persons enumerated. By 1900 inquiries regarding parents' birthplaces, marital status, children born and living, educational status, and home ownership were all added. Note that the census of 1890 was completely destroyed by a fire in the Commerce building in 1920.

Individual military records remain sealed for seventy-five years after the end of service. They are in the custody of the respective branches of the military in Washington, D.C.

Immigration records are held in the Library of Congress and contain the names, dates, and country of origin for immigrants entering the U.S. There is no direct public access and information is by special request only.

International Sources

Lloyd's Register of Shipping, 71 Fenchurch Street, London, has, since 1764, compiled annual registers of all merchant ship voyages in the world. Information includes the names of owners, the place and date the ship was built, its tonnage and dimensions, official number and call sign, and—from 1764 to 1873—the ship's registered destination. Information is available upon request.

Interpol

Interpol (the International Criminal Police Commission) was founded in 1923 following the Second International Judicial Police Conference, convened to discuss the rapid rise in international crime since the World War. Located in Vienna, Austria, Interpol facilitates cooperation between different national police forces faced with apprehending smugglers, counterfeiters, and other criminals that operate across national borders. Each affiliated country has a clearing house through which individual police forces communicate with the general secretariat.

Interpol maintains a register of known international criminals including lists of known associates, aliases, modus operandi, and a rapidly expanding fingerprint file. Information is passed through confidential circulars to police forces in affiliated countries. There is no public access to Interpol files; all requests must be made through an affiliated police force.

Newspapers

NEWSPAPERS HAVE BEEN in existence for centuries, and dailies and weeklies are printed in every corner of the globe, in nearly every language known to man. Breaking stories can be followed, or events that took place decades ago can be traced and discovered. Newspaper offices maintain complete files of earlier editions, kept in 'the morgue.' Many universities and libraries maintain complete files of local and regional newspapers.

Clipping Services

The use of a professional clipping service may be desired. These companies maintain multiple subscriptions to many newspapers and magazines and, for a fee, clip articles of interest to their clients. Initial fees are small, ranging from $1.50 to $4.00 a week, increasing with the number of topics added to the client's list. Outlets in places like New York City provide services for foreign language newspapers, employing a battery of translators to search the periodicals for information desired by their clients. Personal correspondents living in other parts of the country or world are also a good source of interesting clippings.

Maintaining Files

Maintaining control of a collection of clippings is not easy. Many will cross-reference to books in the investigator's library or to other sources. Taking full advantage of a large and ever-growing collection of disjointed bits of information takes some work. A month of full or part-time application to the task results in a workable system that provides a percentage chance of providing useful information equal to the total of the investigator's INT and EDU. This score may be increased by as much as one point per month—if the keeper rules that the investigator has spent the requisite time clipping, collecting, and filing—but can never exceed the investigator's personal Library Use score. It is, of course, up to the keeper whether a personal file holds specific information of value or not.

Cabinet Style Radio

Newspapers From Around the Globe

THE FOLLOWING SELECTION of major newspapers is listed by continent and country. Some include founding dates, language, or other pertinent data. Investigators may subscribe to any of these papers, although those shipped by sea may be weeks or months in transit.

North America

United States

Alabama: *Birmingham Post.*

Arizona: *Phoenix Republic* (1850).

California: *Los Angeles Examiner; Los Angeles Herald; Los Angeles Times* (1881); *Oakland Post-Enquirer; Orange County Register* (1905); *Sacramento Bee* (1857); *San Diego Sun; San Francisco Call; San Diego Union* (1868); *San Francisco Chronicle* (1865); *San Francisco Examiner; San Francisco News.*

Colorado: *Denver Evening News; Denver Rocky Mountain News* (1859).

Florida: *Miami Herald* (1910); *Orlando Sentinel* (1876); *Tampa Tribune* (1893).

Georgia: *Atlanta Constitution* (1868); *Atlanta Georgian-American.*

Illinois: *Chicago Herald & Examiner; Chicago American; Chicago Tribune* (1847); *Evansville Press.*

Indiana: *Indianapolis Times; Terre Haute Post.*

Kentucky: *Covington Kentucky Post.*

Louisiana: *New Orleans Times-Picayune* (1837).

Massachusetts: *Boston Advertiser; Boston American; Boston Globe* (1872); *Boston Herald* (1892); *Christian Science Monitor* (1908).

Maryland: *Baltimore American; Baltimore News; Baltimore Post; Baltimore Sun* (1837).

Michigan: *Detroit Times; Detroit News* (1873); *Detroit Free Press* (1831).

Minnesota: *Minneapolis Star Tribune* (1867).

Missouri: *Kansas City Star* (1880); *St. Louis Post-Dispatch* (1878).

New Jersey: *Newark Star-Ledger* (1832).

New Mexico: *Albuquerque New Mexico State Tribune.*

New York: *Albany Times-Union; Buffalo News* (1880); *New York American; New York Daily Times* (1919); *New York Journal; New York Post* (1801); *New York Telegram; New York Times* (1851); *Rochester Journal; Syracuse Journal; The Wall Street Journal* (1889).

Ohio: *Akron Times-Press; Cincinnati Post; Cleveland Plain Dealer* (1842); *Cleveland Press; Columbus Citizen; Columbus Dispatch* (1871); *Toledo News-Bee; Youngstown Telegram.*

Oklahoma: *Oklahoma City News.*

Oregon: *Portland Oregonian* (1850).

Pennsylvania: *Philadelphia Inquirer* (1829); *Pittsburgh Press; Pittsburgh Sun-Telegraph.*

Tennessee: *Knoxville New-Sentinel;*

Memphis Press-Scimitar.

Texas: *Dallas Morning News* (1882); *El Paso Post; Fort Worth Press; Fort Worth Star-Telegram* (1906); *Houston Chronicle* (1901); *Houston Post* (1885); *Houston Press; San Antonio Light.*

Washington: *Seattle Post-Intelligencer.*

Washington, D.C.: *Washington Herald; Washington News; Washington Post* (1877); *Washington Times.*

Wisconsin: *Milwaukee News; Milwaukee Sentinel* (1837).

Canada

The Halifax Chronicle; La Press (Montreal—French); *The Manitoba Free Press; The Montreal Star; The Montreal Gazette; The Toronto Globe; The Vancouver Daily Province.*

Mexico

Diaro de Yucatan (Merida, 1918); *El Correo del la Tarde* (Mazatlan, 1885); *El Excelsior* (Mexico City, 1919); *El Informador* (Guadalajara, 1917); *El Universal* (Mexico City, 1916); *El Universal Grafico* (Mexico City, 1922); *La Tribuna* (Guaymas, 1926).

South and Central America

Argentina: *El Diario* (Buenos Aires, 1881—evening); *La Nacion* (Buenos Aires, 1870); *La Prensa* (Buenos Aires, 1869); *La Razon* (Buenos Aires, 1905—evening); *The Herald* (Buenos Aires, 1876—English); *The Standard* (Buenos Aires, 1861—English).

Brazil: *A Noite* (Rio de Janeiro, 1910—evening); *A Patria* (Rio de Janeiro, 1920); *Correio de Manha* (Rio de Janeiro, 1902); *Fanfulla* (Sao Paulo, 1892—Italian); *Journal do Commercio* (Rio de Janeiro, 1827); *O Diario de Pernambuco* (1825); *O Estado* (Sao Paulo, 1876); *O Paiz* (Rio de Janeiro, 1884).

Chile: *El Diario Ilustrado* (Santiago); *El Mercurio* (Valparaiso/Santiago/Antofagasta, 1827); *La Union* (Valparaiso/Santiago, 1885); *La Nacion* (Santiago, 1916).

Peru: *El Comercio* (Lima, 1839); *La Cronica* (Lima, 1912); *La Prensa* (Lima, 1903).

Europe

Austria: *Neue Freie Presse; Neues Wiener Journal.*

Belgium: *Het Laatste Nieuws* (Brussels, 1888); *La Derniere Heure* (Brussels, 1906); *Le Peuple* (socialist); *La Libre Belgique* (Brussels, 1884); *Le Soir* (Brussels, 1887).

Czechoslovakia: *Prager Press* (German, government-controlled).

Denmark: *B.T.* (Copenhagen, 1916); *Berlingske Tidende* (Copenhagen, 1749); *Ekstra Bladet* (Copenhagen, 1904); *Politiken* (Copenhagen, 1884).

England (London): *The Daily Chronicle* (1877); *The Daily Express* (1900); *The Daily Mail* (1896); *The Daily Mirror* (1903); *The Daily Telegraph* (1855); *The Financial Times* (1880); *The Evening Standard; The Guardian* (1821); *The Morning Post* (1772); *News of the World* (1843); *The Observer* (1791); *The People* (1881); *The Sunday Express; The Sunday News* (1842); *The Sunday Times* (1822); *The Times* (1785).

England (others): *Birmingham Evening Dispatch; Birmingham Gazette; Bradford Telegraph and Argus; Hull Daily Mail; Grimsby Telegraph; Lanca-*

shire Daily Post; Lincolnshire Chronicle; Liverpool Courier and Express; Liverpool Echo; Nottingham Evening News; Nottingham Journal; Northern Echo (Darlington); Sheffield Independent; Sheffield Mail; Yorkshire Evening News; Yorkshire Gazette; Yorkshire Observer.

France: Echo de Paris; Journal; International Herald Tribune (Paris, 1887); Le Figaro (Paris, 1828); L'Humanite (Paris, 1904); Le Matin; Le Petit Journal; Petit Parisien.

Germany: Berliner Zeitung (1877); Borsen Zeitung (Berlin); Dusseldorfer Nachricthen (1792); Frankfurter General-Anzeiger; Frankfurter Zeitung; Hamburger Anzeiger; Janaische Zeitung (1674); Kolnische Zeitung (1848); Lokal Anzeiger (Berlin).

Hungary: Az Est (Magyar); Pester Lloyd (Budapest, 1858—German); Pesti Hirlap (Magyar).

Ireland: The Dublin Evening Mail; The Irish Independent (Dublin, 1905—morning); The Evening Herald (Dublin, 1894); The Irish Times (Dublin, 1859—morning); The Sunday Independent (Dublin, 1905).

Italy: Corriere della Sera (Milan, 1876); Il Messagero (Rome 1878); Mattino (Naples); La Stampa (Turin, 1867).

Luxembourg: Luxemburger Wort—La Voix du Luxembourg (1848).

Netherlands: Algemeen Handelsblad (Amsterdam); De Telegraaf (Amsterdam, 1893); De Volksrant (Amsterdam, 1919); Nieuwe Rotterdamsche Courant.

Portugal: Diario de Noticias (Lisbon, 1864); Diaris Noticia (Lisbon, 1820); Jornaldo Commercio (Lisbon).

Scotland: Edinburgh Evening News; The Glasgow Herald (1783); The Scotsman (Edinburgh, 1817); The Sunday Post (Dundee, 1920).

Spain: ABC (Madrid, 1905); Heraldo (Madrid); Liberal (Madrid); El Sol (1917); La Vanguardia (Barcelona, 1881).

Switzerland: Journal de Geneve (French); Neue Zurcher Zeitung (German); Zurcher Post (German).

Asia

China: The Central China Post (Hankow—British); The China Mail (Hong Kong—British, evening); The China Press (Shanghai—American, daily); The Hong Kong Daily Express (British); The Hong Kong Telegraph (British, evening); Le Journal de Pekin (French, morning); L'Echo de Chine (Shanghai—French, morning); L'Echo de Tientsin (French, morning); The North China Daily Mail (Tientsin—British, evening); North China Daily News (Shanghai, 1864—British); The North China Star (Tientsin—American, morning); The Peking Leader (American, morning); The Peking and Tientsin Times (British); The Shanghai Mercury (British, evening); The Shanghai Times (British); The South China Morning Post (Hong Kong—British).

India: The Civil and Military Gazette (Lahore—British); The Englishman (Calcutta, 1821—British); The Madras Mail (British); The Pioneer (Allhabad—British); The Statesman (Calcutta—British); The Times of India (Bombay—British).

Japan: The Japan Advertiser (American); The Japan Chronicle (British); The Japan Times (Japanese owned, printed in English); Osaka Asahi; Osaka Mainichi; Tokyo Asahi; Tokyo Nichinichi.

Russia: Izvestia (Moscow); Kranaya Gazeta (Leningrad); Pravda.

Africa and Australia

South Africa: Die Burger (Cape Town—Dutch); The Cape Argus; The Cape Times; The Johannesburg Star; Ons Land (Cape Town—Dutch); Volkstem (Pretoria—Dutch).

Australia: The Age (Melbourne—morning); The Argus (Melbourne—morning); The Daily Guardian (Sydney); The Sydney Morning Herald.

American Magazines

Atlantic Monthly, Century, Collier's, Cosmopolitan, Fortune, The Forum, Good Housekeeping, Harper's, Hearst's International Magazine, Ladies' Home Journal, Life, Modern Electronics, New Yorker (1925), North American Review, Reader's Digest (1922), The Ring, Saturday Evening Post, Scribner's, Time, Vanity Fair, Variety, Vogue.

Press Associations

INVESTIGATORS MAY WISH to pursue breaking national and international stories directly through a press agency. There are two in the U.S., Associated Press (AP) and United Press International (UPI). Both gather factual, up-to-the-minute news for newspapers and other media subscribers. Service is not usually offered to private parties, nor are agency files open to the public. Investigators may have to develop their own contacts.

Associated Press is a non-profit cooperative based in New York. It was founded in 1848 by six New York newspaper publishers wishing to share the costs of long distance news gathering. Before the days of telegraph, radio, and ticker tapes, AP collected information by culling newspapers from overseas. United Press International is privately owned. Founded in 1907, it is also based in New York.

The two major press agencies in Europe are Reuters, founded in Europe in 1849, now headquartered in London, and Agence Havas in Paris, founded 1832.

OTHER PRESS AGENCIES

ALD Agencia Los Diarios; Buenos Aires, Argentina (1910).

ANA Athenagence; Athens, Greece (1896).

AUP Australian United Press; Melbourne, Australia (1928).

BELGA Agence Belga; Brussels, Belgium (1920).

BTA Bulgarska Telegrafitscheka; Sofia, Bulgaria (1898).

CNA Central News Agency; Taipei (1924).

CP Canadian Press; Toronto, Canada (1917).

CTK Ceskoslovenka Tiskova Kancelar; Prague, Czechoslovakia (1918).

EXTEL Exchange and Telegraph Company; London, England (1872).

FIDES Agenzia Internationale Fides; Vatican City, Italy (1926).

JTA Jewish Telegraphic Agency; Jerusalem, Palestine (1919).

NTB Norsk Telegrambyra; Oslo, Norway (1867).

NZPA New Zealand Press Agency; Wellington, New Zealand (1879).

PA Press Association; London, England (1868).

PS Presse Service; Paris, France (1929).

RB Ritzaus Bureau; Copenhagen, Denmark (1866).

SDA Schweizerische Depeschenagentur; Berne, Switzerland (1894).

TASS Telegraph Agency of the Sovereign State; Moscow, Russia (1925).

Libraries and Museums

ALL BUT THE SMALLEST of American communities have some sort of public library. Big cities pride themselves on the size of their public libraries; colleges and universities usually allow public access to their collections. But specialized problems often call for specialized research and local libraries may not have what the investigator needs or wants. Listed below are some of the best known and most complete libraries and museums in the country.

American Museum of Natural History

New York City, New York

Located on Central Park West at 79th Street, the museum is housed in a red brick gothic structure built in 1877. It is open to the public from 10 AM to 5:45 PM every day, and until 9 PM on Wednesdays, Fridays, and Saturdays.

First established in 1869, the American is currently the world's largest natural history museum, encompassing all areas of natural history and anthropology, save botany. The museum's unique displays of mounted birds, mammals, fish, and reptiles were pioneered by Carl Akeley in the early part of the decade. The museum has a standing agreement with New York's Central Park Zoo, accepting from them animal carcasses of all sorts. They also accept donations of rare animal carcasses from private parties. The basement taxidermy laboratory is often the source of strange odors that permeate the exhibition halls. The museum boasts more complete skeletons of extinct animals on display—particularly dinosaurs—than any museum in the world. The museum was the first to display articulated dinosaur skeletons, and later to perfect the techniques of mounting animals realistically using glass, wax, and other materials.

The museum backs many expeditions, including the Arctic explorations of Robert Peary in 1890s and early 1900s. The 'Ahnighito,' the world's largest known meteorite, discovered by Peary in Greenland, is on display in the foyer. Elsewhere is the mounted skeleton of an Eskimo, one of six brought back by Peary, and one of the four who soon after succumbed to tuberculosis.

In 1902, when the eruption of Mt. Pelee killed 30,000 people on the island of Martinique in the West Indies, the museum mounted a field expedition to climb the still erupting volcano. Later, Carl Akeley, the museum's taxidermist, undertook three expeditions to Africa.

A ten-year Asiatic expedition mounted between 1920 and 1930 was headquartered in Peking. An army of explorers, paleontologists, archaeologists, zoologists, geologists, and surgeons made trips into Mongolia exploring the Gobi desert, surviving bandit attacks and hostile terrain. The first known fossil dinosaur eggs were discovered during this period by paleontologist Roy Chapman Andrews. Early reports that claimed to have discovered evidence of a prehistoric civilization of an Asian plateau were later refuted, although never satisfactorily explained.

The museum receives many applications from people wanting to accompany expeditions. Such inquiries are answered with a standard form with the question: "Could you donate to the expedition a sum of money to help pay your expenses?" With enough money, almost anyone can join an expedition.

Harvard University

Cambridge, Massachusetts

Harvard is America's oldest and most prestigious university. Founded in 1636 as a Puritan college for the education of ministers, it was named after John Harvard who, in 1638, bequeathed his entire library and half his estate to the school. Only a single volume of Harvard's library survives to this day: John Downham's *The Christian Warfare Against the Devill World and Flesh*, published in 1634. Most of the original collection perished when in January, 1764, Harvard Hall was struck by lightning and burned to the ground.

Harvard's library is one of the finest collections in America with over 2,785,000 books and pamphlets on catalogue. Although intended for the use of students and faculty, the permission of a librarian grants an individual access to the different collections. The university also features a botanical garden, an observatory, museums of European, Oriental, and American art, the Semitic museum, and the German museum.

The Peabody Museum of American Archaeology and Ethnology, founded 1866, was the first anthropological museum in the U.S. Although it originally focused on the New World, it has since expanded its interests to encompass the whole of the globe. Since 1891 the Peabody has conducted extensive explorations of Mayan ruins in Central America. On file is a complete collection of nearly every anthropological journal ever published—over 20,000 issues.

In 1915 the Widener Library was added to help house the university's ever-growing collection. Named after Henry Widener, a Harvard student (and millionaire) who died aboard the Titanic, it contains rare volumes by Luther, Erasmus, and Machiavelli.

Harvard also maintains an astronomical observatory in Arequipa, Peru, which, in 1927, is moved to South Africa.

Research & Resources

Miskatonic University

Arkham, Massachusetts

Located in the city of Arkham, Massachusetts, the small Miskatonic University is rightly famed for its library. Its collection is comparatively small, holding about 400,000 titles, but has been carefully assembled and well chosen. The Miskatonic Library is particularly strong in the areas of Medieval History and Metaphysics, and has a fine collection of 17th and 18th century volumes.

The university's Exhibit Museum is open to the public. It boasts one of the region's best collections of American Indian artifacts, Early American handicrafts, and New England witchcraft.

National Geographic Society

Washington, D.C.

The Society was founded in 1888 by an eminent group of explorers and scientists "for the increase and diffusion of geographic knowledge". In the same year it commenced publication of *National Geographic* magazine, sent to all members of the society. In January, 1905, the magazine began publishing photo-features, the first of Lhasa, the mysterious holy city of Tibet. Color was introduced five years later. By 1926 circulation exceeded one million copies.

The Society has supported numerous expeditions, often in cooperation with the Smithsonian Institute. The first National Geographic expedition took place in 1890-91 with the exploration and mapping of Mount St. Elias along the then-unknown border between Alaska and Canada. In conjunction with Yale, a Geographic-backed expedition discovered Machu Picchu in 1911 and, later, Pueblo Bonito in New Mexico. The society has also backed several polar expeditions.

The Society has laid the foundations of a tree-ring calendar used to develop a chronology of prehistoric America, predating its European discovery by several centuries.

The Society maintains a select library of over 16,000 volumes maintained by a staff of four. Although public access is not normally allowed, a librarian may offer to help a dedicated researcher. Aside from books, the library contains many unpublished manuscripts and journals from different expeditions, and a complete run of *Na-*

Other Notable Libraries and Museums

Baltimore Museum of Art, Baltimore, Maryland: Particularly strong in East Indian metal and Cypriote antiquities.

Buffalo Society of Natural Sciences, Buffalo, New York: Strong in fossil invertebrates of the Devonian period.

California Academy of Sciences, San Francisco, California: Specializes in flora and fauna of the Pacific Coast and Western states. Very rich in reptiles, particularly Galapagos tortoises.

California, University of, Berkeley, California: 665,680 volumes.

Carnegie Institute, Pittsburgh, Pennsylvania: Features a library, fine arts, museum, music, a library school, and displays of technology. The museum has a large collection of fossil vertebrates, South American birds, and butterflies—especially African. There is also a large collection of coins and medals.

Chicago Field Museum, Chicago, Illinois: Specializes in birds of North and South America, and mammals of the Americas and Africa. The Field museum has the largest collection of meteorites in the world and the best botany collection in the U.S.

Chicago, University of, Chicago, Illinois: 768,559 volumes.

Cincinnati Museum Association, Cincinnati, Ohio: 30,000 specimens of American Indian archaeology and ethnology.

Colorado Museum of Natural History, Denver, Colorado: Specializes in fossil vertebrates.

Columbia University, New York, New York: 1,092,343 volumes.

Cornell University, Ithaca, New York: 787,127 volumes.

Crear Library, Chicago, Illinois: 820,000 volumes.

Enoch Pratt Free Library, Baltimore, Maryland.

Illinois, University of, Champaign, Illinois: 708,850 volumes.

Michigan, University of, Ann Arbor, Michigan: 649,912 volumes.

Minnesota, University of, Minneapolis-St. Paul, Minnesota: 501,507 volumes.

Museum of the Academy of Natural Sciences of Philadelphia, Philadelphia, Pennsylvania: Zoology and paleontology. The largest collection of mollusks in U.S.

Museum of the American Indian, New York, New York: Has over two million exhibits, one-quarter of them on display at any given time. Known for field work, publications, and monographs.

New York Public Library, New York, New York: World's largest public library with over 2,971,000 books and pamphlets. Formed from the Astor (1849), Lenox (1870), and Tilden (1892) libraries.

New York State Museum, Albany, New York: Specializes in flora and fauna of the state, as well as extensive historical collections.

Newberry Library, Chicago, Illinois: 443,757 books and pamphlets.

Peabody Maritime Museum, Salem, Massachusetts. East India trade and whaling are specialties.

Peabody Museum of Yale, New Haven, Connecticut: Very strong in fossil vertebrates, particularly dinosaurs. An outstanding collection of early, toothed birds, and primitive horses.

Pennsylvania, University of, Philadelphia, Pennsylvania: 635,070 volumes.

Princeton University, Princeton, New Jersey: 594,195 volumes.

Toledo Museum of Art, Toledo, Ohio: The world's largest collection of ancient glass, and a notable collection of early printed books.

U.S. Natural History Museum, Washington, D.C.: Mineral and mollusc collections are first rate. Features a technology museum.

Yale University Library, New Haven, Connecticut: 1,838,099 volumes.

tional Geographic magazine. Back issues can be purchased for nominal fees.

Smithsonian Institute

Washington, D.C.

The Smithsonian boasts the largest museum and art collection in the world. The various museums and libraries are open to the public on a daily basis, 10 AM to 5 PM, but research facilities are only available to those authorized by the Institute. The Smithsonian park covers nine city blocks and five different buildings.

The Smithsonian was founded in 1829 when British scientist James Smithson died leaving a proviso in his will to the effect that should his inheriting nephew die without heir, the fortune should go to the United States "to found an establishment for the increase and diffusion of knowledge." The U.S. government received the money in 1838, soon after establishing an act providing for a library and museum to contain "objects of art, and of foreign and curious research."

The red sandstone, gothic-style building was completed in 1855 and soon after dubbed "the Castle." It originally contained a public exhibition area, offices, laboratories, and sleeping quarters for visiting scientists. The Institute's first secretary, Joseph Henry, was primarily interested in research and scientific advancement, and between 1846 and 1870 the Institute was heavily engaged in meteorological studies. Later, the study of North American archaeology and ethnology was stressed. An international exchange of scientific literature was arranged and the Institute began promoting itself through the publication of periodicals and monographs on specialist subjects.

In 1858 the National Cabinet of Curiosities was transferred to the Castle from the Patent House. In 1881 a second building was constructed to house the exhibits from the earlier United States International Exposition. Originally called the United States National museum, it was later renamed the Arts and Industries Building. A small astronomical observatory was added in 1890, the Natural History building in 1911, and the Freer Gallery of Art in 1923.

The Institute's displays include natural history, industry, art, technology and science, rare gems, history and ethnology. The large library is particularly complete in the areas of Far and Near Eastern art and literature.

In 1904 James Smithson's body was exhumed and transported to the United States. It is now interred in a small chamber in the Castle known as the Crypt Room.

U.S. Library of Congress

Washington, D.C.

Originally established in 1800 to serve congress, the first library was destroyed by invading British in 1814. Thomas Jefferson offered his personal library of 6,487

books as a replacement, a collection still intact and found in the Rare Book and Special Collection Division. Although a second fire in 1851 destroyed nearly two-thirds of the library's collection, by 1927 the library holds 3,556,767 books and pamphlets, a collection only eclipsed by the British Museum in London, and the Bibliotheque Nationale in Paris.

The library received its biggest boost in 1864 when it was expanded and opened to the public by Ainsworth Spofford, who also arranged for the library to receive two free copies of every book, map, chart, musical composition, engraving, and photograph submitted for copyright. He also arranged for a scientific material exchange with the neighboring Smithsonian Institute.

A new building featuring a domed reading room 125 feet across was completed in 1897, making the library the largest, costliest, and most ornate in the world; floor space amounts to more than 13 1/2 acres. Herbert Putnam was soon after named librarian and he instituted a classification system now used by libraries everywhere. In 1921, important State Department documents were transferred to the Library of Congress and it was during this time that Putnam was able to gain almost unlimited funds, which he used to acquire rare books and artifacts. Among its most valuable holdings are a 1455 Gutenberg Bible, a collection of early presidential manuscripts, and the world's largest collection of miniature books. The library is strongest in bibliography, history, political and social sciences, law and legislation, fine arts, American local history, biography, and genealogy. During the 1920s the Library of Congress served as the nation's archives.

Open to the public Monday through Friday from 8:30 AM till 9 PM, Saturday from 8:30 AM till 5 PM, and Sundays from 1 PM till 5 PM.

Overseas Libraries of Note

British Museum, London, England

In 1929 the library held over 3,200,000 printed volumes and over 56,000 manuscripts. A unique and extensive collection of newspapers and journals has been housed in a separate building since 1906.

Bibliotheque Nationale, Paris, France

France's national library was formed from the old Royal Library. It receives a copy of every book published in France, and in 1926 held more than 4,400,000 printed books, over 500,000 maps and plans, nearly 122,000 manuscripts, and many other antiquities as well.

Vatican Apostolic Library, Vatican City, Italy

There are few records of this library prior to the 13th century, but it is believed that the core volumes date back to the earliest Roman pontiffs. ∎

Consultants

AN INVESTIGATOR SEEKING advice may need to interview a professional source. The following is a sample of some of the famous and not-so-famous people active today. Some may prove too important or too busy to answer letters from strangers; others may show a distinct interest. Intrusive telephone calls or unannounced visits may prove counter-productive.

EVANGELINE ADAMS (1865-1932), astrologer

THE leading astrologer in the U.S., Adams resides in a New York City apartment above Carnegie Hall. Her reputation was made in 1899 when she accurately prophesied the burning of New York's Windsor Hotel. Prosecuted for fortune telling in 1914, she so impressed the judge with the accuracy of her readings that he dropped the charges. Author of the best-seller, Astrology: Your Place Among the Stars, she begins a popular radio program in 1930.

Adams regularly accepts appointments for astrological readings.

ROY CHAPMAN ANDREWS (1884-1960), explorer, naturalist, paleontologist

ANDREWS was born in Wisconsin and graduated from Beloit College in 1906. He immediately went to work for the American Museum of Natural History in New York securing whale specimens, and soon became a leading world expert on those great sea mammals.

Andrews also took part in expeditions to the northwest coast of North America in 1908, to Indonesia in 1909-10, and Korea in 1911. He trekked through northern Korea in 1911-12, Alaska in 1912, southwestern China and Burma in 1916, northern China and Outer Mongolia in 1919, and spent most of the decade between 1920 and 1930 in central Asia. It was during his stay in China in 1918 that Andrews also worked for the U.S. Intelligence Bureau in an unspecified capacity. Among the many discoveries he has made are the first fossil dinosaur eggs ever found.

Andrews has had many books published including: Whale Hunting with Gun and Camera (1916), Camps and Trails in China (1918), Across Mongolian Plains (1921), On the Trail of An-

cient Man (1926), and Ends of the Earth (1929).

In and out of the country, Andrews can usually be contacted through the American Natural History Museum in New York. Andrews is in regular contact by radio and through mail drops.

RICHARD E. BYRD (1888-1957), military officer, pilot, polar explorer

AN acclaimed naval officer and polar explorer, Byrd is a member of a prominent Virginia family (his brother was governor in the late 1920s). He attended the Virginia Military Institute, the University of Virginia, and the US. Naval Academy. He later trained as a pilot, commanding aviation units in Canada, navigating the Navy's first transatlantic flight in 1919, and commanding the aviation unit of the MacMillan polar expedition in Greenland in 1925. On May 9, 1926, accompanied by copilot Floyd Bennett, Byrd flies over the north pole, covering 1360 miles on a fifteen-hour flight.

In 1928 Byrd leads a lengthy expedition to the Antarctic where he establishes a base camp called Little America. In late November of 1929, he and three companions fly over the South Pole. He returns to America a national hero, and publishes a memoir of the expedition titled, Little America. Byrd later makes other expeditions to the south polar regions.

Byrd is the author of Skyward (1928), and Little America (1930).

EDGAR CAYCE (1878?-1945), mystic, prophet, healer

A KENTUCKY-born mystic and psychic healer, Cayce's background is rural, his education limited, and his demeanor unassuming. He claims he first became aware of his powers in 1890 when a ghostly woman approached him and offered to grant a single wish. Answering that he only wished to help others, he afterwards began to exhibit psychic powers. Known as "the sleeping prophet," Cayce is a devout Christian who never seems at ease with his gifts.

Cayce provides his patients with thousands of psychic readings in the early part of the 20th century. Entering a self-induced trance, he dictates prophecies and medical diagnoses for afflicted

persons, sometimes at great distance from the supplicants. Although his recommendations frequently call for bizarre home remedies, many of his patients have reported miraculous cures. His explorations of people's psyches have provided evidence of the existence of past lives.

He dislikes accepting money for his services, but many of his patients are generous. In 1923 he abandons his career in photography to make a living with his psychic talents. Cayce claims his knowledge comes from "the akashic records," a psychic storehouse of knowledge not dissimilar to Carl Jung's theory of the collective unconscious. Cayce calls this storehouse "God's book of remembrance," or "the universal unconscious." He often refers to Atlantis, and claims a storehouse of Atlantean knowledge is contained in secret libraries beneath the Egyptian pyramids.

Cayce accepts personal appointments, or can be contacted by letter.

CLARENCE DARROW (1857-1938), jurist

BORN in Ohio, Darrow was admitted to the bar in 1878 and moved to Chicago in 1887. He immediately became involved in the trials following the Haymarket riots of 1886, defending anarchists charged with murder. In 1890 Darrow was appointed counsel for the Chicago City Corporation, later serving as general attorney for the North Western Railway. He left the railway to defend Communist Eugene Debs and other members of the railway union on contempt of court charges stemming from the Pullman strike of 1894. Although he lost the case, it established Darrow's national reputation as a labor and criminal lawyer. In 1903 he was appointed arbitrator of the Pennsylvania coal strikes by Teddy Roosevelt and, in 1907, obtained the acquittal of William "Big Bill" Haywood, charged with the assassination of Idaho governor Frank Steunenberg. Darrow abandoned labor litigation in 1911 after the two men he was defending against charges of dynamiting the Los Angeles Times building unexpectedly switched their pleas to "guilty" in the midst of the trial.

After the War, Darrow defended members of Bill Thompson's corrupt Chicago city government, then in 1924,

Leopold and Loeb, accused of the murder of Bobby Franks. In 1925 Darrow made his biggest mark, defending Tennessee school teacher John T. Scopes, accused of teaching Darwinian evolution. Darrow was opposed by famed orator William Jennings Bryan, and although Darrow lost the contest, his incisive questioning of traditional Biblical teachings was considered a victory for rational, scientific thinking. In 1925-26 Darrow conducts the Sweet case in Detroit, winning acquittal for a black family forced to defend itself against a mob trying to run them out of the neighborhood.

Darrow has published *Crime: Its Cause and Treatment* (1922), and *The Prohibition Mania* (1927, with Victor S. Yarrow).

Darrow lives and maintains an office in Chicago, Illinois. He is particularly fond of high-profile, headline-grabbing cases.

THOMAS EDISON
(1847-1931), inventor, scientist

EDISON, best known for his invention of the incandescent light bulb and the motion picture, was the foremost American inventor of the late 19th century. Holder of hundreds of patents, Edison has been awarded numerous international honors. In 1928 receives an American Congressional Gold Medal.

As a youth, he worked at various railroad occupations before starting his own small newspaper and was later employed as a telegraph operator. Lacking formal schooling, Edison nonetheless made many improvements to the telegraph system, and to the stock ticker-tape system. Eventually he set up laboratories in the New Jersey cities of Newark, Menlo Park, and West Orange, where devices such as the phonograph and electrical storage battery were invented and refined.

Edison's creativity is matched only by his capacity for work. Twelve and fourteen-hour days are the norm, and he never trusts his results until they have been proven time and time again. He is close friends with auto tycoon and philanthropist, Henry Ford, who once worked for the inventor.

Edison currently resides near West Orange, New Jersey.

CHARLES FORT
(1874-1932), author, weirdo

FORT is a collector and chronicler of all things strange and bizarre. His penchant for collecting clippings and noting odd occurrences from all over the world results in his first book, *The Book of the Damned*, published in 1919. Within its pages are tales of frogs, stones, and blood raining from the sky, of unexplained daytime darknesses, mysterious flying craft, and inexplicable shadows. An amateur naturalist and professional news reporter, Fort hopes that his books will make scientists pay attention to the many odd and uncorrelated events continually occurring around the globe. A second book, *New Lands*, appears in 1923.

Fort is a solitary soul, living in an apartment in the Bronx of New York with his wife, Anna. Heavyset, and with poor eyesight, Fort has few friends, although novelist Theodore Dreiser is a frequent visitor. The cramped apartment is filled with Fort's cryptically labeled notes and clippings along with his collections of insect specimens and various odd objects gathered from all over the world. Intolerant of science's disregard for the weird and unexplained, he nonetheless sports a quick sense of humor, illegally brews his own beer, and has found time to create a maddeningly difficult game called Super-Checkers.

ROBERT GODDARD
(1882-1945), scientist, inventor

AN early pioneer of rocket science, Goddard's first experiments date to 1909 in his hometown of Worcester, Massachusetts. Goddard attended Worcester Polytechnic Institute and Clark University, later teaching physics at Clark. His ongoing experiments with rocketry, at first funded with his own money, are eventually granted funds by the Smithsonian Institute and the Guggenheims. In 1919 Goddard publishes *A Method of Reaching Extreme Altitudes*, outlining a rocket design intended to reach the moon. The book is met with scorn but he continues his studies undismayed. On March 16, 1926, at Auburn, Massachusetts, he successfully launches his first liquid-fuel rocket.

Goddard is employed as a physics professor at Clark University in Worcester, Massachusetts.

WILLIAM RANDOLPH HEARST
1863-1951), newspaper tycoon

HEARST was born and raised in San Francisco, California, the only son of George Hearst, gold mine owner and U.S. Senator from California from 1886-1891. Hearst was educated at Harvard, eventually deciding on a career in journalism. Following the example of Joseph Pulitzer and his *New York World*, Hearst, in 1897, took control of the struggling *San Francisco Examiner* and within two years showed a profit.

He then moved into the New York market, purchasing the struggling *Morning Journal*, hiring such writers as Stephen Crane and Julian Hawthorne, and raiding Pulitzer's staff for people like Richard F. Outcault, the inventor of color comics. Renamed the *Journal-American*, Hearst dropped the price to one cent, added illustrations, and made good use of sensational headlines. Hearst used his papers to excoriate Britain during the 1895 Venezuela-British Guiana border dispute, and has been accused of using his newspapers to stir up the Spanish-American War in an effort to increase sales.

Hearst supported presidential candidate William Jennings Bryan in the elections of 1896 and 1900. A Hearst editorial in early 1901 that advocated assassination as a political tool caused considerable embarrassment when President McKinley was assassinated five months later. Hearst served in Congress from 1903-07, and was unsuccessful in his 1904 presidential nomination bid. In 1905 he barely lost the New York City mayoral race, in 1906 failed to gain the New York governor's seat, and in 1909 again lost the mayoral election, finally ending his political career.

A strict isolationist, Hearst opposed U.S. entry into the World War and later, membership in the League of Nations. His attacks against Britain and France led to these two nations refusing to allow his newspapers access to these nation's communication systems.

By 1925 Hearst owns newspapers all over the country, as well as several magazines. Later he turns to film, producing several movies, some starring his mistress, actress Marion Davies. He has begun construction of Hearst Castle in San Simeon, California, and is presently furnishing it with extravagant antiques and works of art purchased on a lavish scale.

The depression of the 1930s takes its toll on the Hearst empire, but he maintains his influence in the Democratic party, contributing heavily to the nomination of Franklin Delano Roosevelt in 1932.

Hearst is fond of sensational news stories, and has no qualms about publicizing the efforts of a single, crusading journalist. Hearst is also a philanthropist, donating large sums of money to charities and scientific endeavors. He is also in the market for works of art and other exotica with which to furnish Hearst Castle.

J. EDGAR HOOVER
(1895-1972), Director of the FBI

HOOVER was born in Washington, D.C. He graduated from Washington Central High in 1913 and began studying law in night school, eventually receiving a bachelor of laws in 1916, and a master of laws in 1917.

Later in 1917 he began work for the Department of Justice, employed as a file reviewer. Two years later he was promoted to the post of special assistant to A. Mitchell Palmer, then Attorney General. Hoover is given credit for organizing the raids and mass arrests of suspected socialists and communists in the early 1920s.

In May of 1924 Hoover was named acting director of the Bureau of Investigation (renamed the Federal Bureau of Investigation in 1927), and was awarded the permanent position seven months later. Finding the agency in disrepute due to the scandals of the Harding administration, Hoover went about refurbishing the Bureau. Rigorous qualifications were put in effect, requiring agents to have a squeaky-clean record, and an intensive training program was established. Hoover also instituted a national fingerprint file and a scientific crime-detection laboratory.

Early recognizing the value of publicity, Hoover turned it to his own ends, establishing the FBI's "Ten Most Wanted List" and other promotional devices. "If there is going to be publicity," Hoover declared, "let it be on the side of law and order." Under Hoover's leadership the FBI became known for its integrity and freedom from political control. It is the 1930s before Hoover and the FBI become nationally recognized, following the pursuit and arrests of John Dillinger, Ma Barker's gang, and Baby-face Nelson, along with involvement in such high-profile crimes as the Lindbergh kidnaping.

Hoover is a patriotic American who fears infiltration by communists, socialists, anarchists, fascists, and radicals. He actively garners intelligence about labor unions, the KKK, the NAACP and others. His secret surveillance extends to politicians, celebrities, and other national figures.

Hoover's offices are located in Washington, D.C. He is very interested in hearing of any cult conspiracies or other underground movements.

HARRY HOUDINI
(1874-1926), showman, escape artist

HARRY Houdini is one of the best-known stage acts in the world. Born Erich Weiss in Budapest, he immigrated to America as a baby. Taking the stage name of Houdini (after the famous French magician of the early 19th century, Jean-Eugene Robert-Houdin), his first act consisted of traditional card tricks, sleight-of-hand, and feats of 'mentalism.' But he soon abandoned these in favor of escape routines. Wriggling free of manacles and strait-jackets, escaping unharmed from sealed milk cans, water-filled boxes, coffins, and even maximum security cells in local jails, Houdini soon gained a reputation that made him a headliner on American vaudeville circuits and in European dance halls.

Houdini's mother died in 1913 and the devoted son took up an interest in spiritualism that lasts until his death. Encountering fraudulent mediums at every turn, he currently uses his illusionist's talents to expose fakes and hustlers, all the while never abandoning his belief in spiritualism.

In 1926, in Detroit, Michigan, he suffers a blow to the stomach from an overeager fan and dies shortly after, on Halloween, a victim of peritonitis. Survived by his wife and assistant of many years, Bess, he has sworn that if at all possible, he will return from the 'other side' on a future Halloween night.

PROFESSOR J.B. RHINE
(1895-1980), parapsychologist

RHINE quits his post at West Virginia University in 1927 to study psychical research under William McDougall at Duke University in Durham, North Carolina. Rhine conducts carefully controlled experiments in telepathy, telekinesis, and clairvoyance, and investigates psychic phenomena in everyday life and religion. He coined the term 'parapsychology' and invents the standard deck of 25 cards marked with five different symbols used to test ESP. In 1930 he is named Director of the Parapsychology Laboratory at Duke. Rhine lives in Durham, near campus.

ROBERT RIPLEY
(1893-1949), cartoonist, columnist

RIPLEY began his career in 1910 as a sports cartoonist working for several newspapers. In 1918 he created the "Believe It or Not!" series of columns, soon after syndicated to newspapers all over the country. Ripley publishes his first collection of columns in Ripley's "Believe It or Not!" in 1930.

Ripley already has accumulated a large collection of strange objects from all over the globe. He receives many unsolicited objects, and may have specimens for comparison, or special knowledge of an odd item or artifact.

Ripley resides in Santa Rosa, California.

WILLIAM SEABROOK
(1886-1945), traveler, author

A POPULAR author of stories and articles about witchcraft and kindred subjects, Seabrook contributes to many American magazines as well as the New York Times. Beginning in 1924 he is in and out of the U.S., traveling extensively in Arabia, Kurdistan, Tripoli, Haiti, and West Africa, studying unusual rituals and beliefs. He describes his experiences in several books published in the 1930s.

When in the U.S., Seabrook lives in the New York area.

NIKOLA TESLA
(1856-1935), scientist, inventor

AN American inventor, born and educated in Europe, Tesla is rarely recognized for his vast contributions to the sciences. Emigrating to America in 1884, he patented an electric motor in 1888 that he soon sold to the George Westinghouse company. In 1891 he developed the Tesla coil, and in 1893 a system for wireless communication. Briefly associated with Thomas Edison, he soon went his own way, establishing a laboratory in New York City.

Tesla's inventive genius is more theoretical than practical, and he often abandons designs before they are fully developed, leaving others to reap the rewards. Such a situation has led to a long court battle over the rights to basic radio patents. He spends his later years attempting to transmit electricity without wires, growing increasingly reclusive and eccentric. Many publicity photos issued by the inventor have been shown to be fakes, and wild claims made in the 1930s, including the announcement of a "death ray," do little to improve his reputation.

PART-3

Transport & Travel

Getting Around Town, The Bicycle, Getting Out of Town, Rail Travel, Automobiles & Others, Choosing an Automobile, Trucks and Buses, Motorcycle, Boats & Others, Air Travel.

ONCE RESEARCH IS COMPLETED, investigation of the scene is usually essential. A wide variety of transportation forms are available to serve the needs of the traveler. Those most important are described below.

Getting Around Town

AS LONG AS AN INVESTIGATION stays confined to a single community, transportation poses little or no problem. Most American towns, even those as small as 5,000 people or less, offer some form of mass transit. In towns or villages smaller than this the investigator finds need of little more than his own two legs.

Buses and Trolleys

Electric trolleys, powered by either overhead wires or rails in the ground, have been around since before the turn of the century and by 1902 replacing horse drawn omnibuses in almost every city. Termed a "light-rail" system, surface-route trolleys are now in danger of being replaced by more efficient and flexible gasoline-powered buses. Despite this, the cities of Boston, Chicago, New York, and Philadelphia all retain extensive systems featuring high-speed routes on elevated tracks or through underground tunnels. Trolley buses, electrically powered buses running from overhead trolley lines, are a halfway step between light rail and buses. Most American buses are single-deck models, although larger cities like New York are making use of double-deck versions.

Fares

Trolley and bus fare before 1920 was 5 cents. By the end of the decade 10 cents is the universal norm. The price allows the rider to travel the length of the line; transfers are available if more than one line is required to reach a destination, costing either 1 or 2 cents. Transfer use is usually limited by date, a certain time period, and/or the number of times used.

Hours of operation are dictated by the needs of the community. Small towns often suspend operation in early evening, after the close of business hours. Larger communities might maintain reduced service until 10 PM or midnight. The largest cities run their transit systems round the clock, increasing and decreasing the number of runs as needs dictate.

Taxi Cabs

Taxi cabs are common to all American towns, large and small. Even communities with as few as 2000 people often have one or two independent operators. Large cities, such as New York, have several cab companies fielding competing fleets. Cab stands, with waiting taxis, are usually found in front of hotels, railway stations, and other such locations. A phone call to the cab company brings a cab to your door, usually within 10-30 minutes.

Radios are not yet common to taxicabs and drivers must contact their dispatchers by phone, or in person. Special telephones linked directly to the cab companies can be found at cab stands, bus stations, or other places. They can be used by drivers or customers.

Taxi Rates

Taxis charge set rates, prescribed by the local community and based on distance traveled and time spent in the cab. Mechanical meters with timers and spring-driven clocks automatically compute the rate. Meters can be tampered and consequently are periodically checked and certified by the local taxi board. Ford and Chevrolet build special versions of their autos for Yellow and Checker, the two largest American taxi companies.

Rates vary, but are generally higher in large cities. Typical is an opening charge of 15 cents (the flag drop), then a distance charge of 5 cents a mile. A clock keeps the meter ticking at a slow pace, even when the taxi is stuck in traffic. A waiting taxi charges $2 an hour.

Taxi drivers service all levels of the community and are often a good source of local information, both general and specific. A tip of 5-10% is considered customary.

The Bicycle

Young, healthy investigators may want to consider a bicycle. Weighing 35 pounds or less, these durable vehicles are capable of safely transporting up to ten times their own weight. Current bicycle design is based on the "safety" model that appeared in the late 19th century and replaced the original "ordinary" design with its gigantic front wheel and tiny rear wheel. Pneumatic tires have been standard for decades and three-speed gear systems were long ago perfected, their range now extended by reversible hubs and cranks featuring different sized sprockets. European bicycles are usually equipped with hand operated, front-rim or caliper-style brakes. American designs favor the rear wheel "coaster" brake, operated by reversing the direction of the pedals.

Skill—Ride Bicycle

ALTHOUGH LONG A favored form of personal transportation, a good many adult-aged investigators may find they never have had the chance to learn how to ride a bike. Unless an investigator's personal history definitely shows otherwise, the character must make a successful halved Luck roll to show he had the good fortune to have owned a bicycle as a child.

Novice riders continue to fall, crash, or otherwise go out of control until they make a successful roll of POW x3 or less. Once achieved. the investigator is awarded a Ride Bicycle skill of 25% and can safely start, stop, and get about without undue risk.

European racing-styled bicycles cost from $50-$100 or more. Some weigh as little as 15 pounds, but they may be limited in use. European designs are intended for the narrow, twisting, paved roads found in cities and on alpine routes. If the investigator intends to spend any time at all on the dirt and gravel back roads of America, the "roadster" style bicycle sold and developed by such U.S. manufacturers as Schwinn and Elgin is recommended. Wide tires, solid and heavy frames, and broad cow-horn style handlebars prevail under conditions where more delicately tuned models are rattled and shaken apart.

A deluxe model American bicycle with steel rims, tool kit with pump, luggage rack, and battery-powered light and horn, costs $40-$50. Cheaper models can be had for under $20. Tandem bicycles, built for two, are still popular. Some have a lowered frame in the second seat to allow for women's skirts.

Motorized Bicycles

Motorized bicycles are a popular choice. Small gasoline engines, usually mounted in the frame or over the front fender, drive the front wheel through a clutched belt. Pedaling is necessary to start the engine, and to assist climbing steeper hills. On level ground a motorized bicycle can cruise at speeds of 15-20 mph.

Licensing

Most cities require the registration and licensing of bicycles, whether motorized or not (a practice generally dropped in the latter half of the century). Operator's licenses are not required.

Bicycle Accessories

Trouser guards are 5 cents a pair; leather hand grips, 27 cents a pair; combination-style sprocketlock, 72 cents; foot pump, 75 cents; deluxe saddle, $1.58; self-installed cyclometer (odometer), 85 cents, or $2.48 for the double-dial model for daily mileage (0-99.9 and 0-9999.9); lighting systems, either electric or acetylene powered, $1.98 to $2.79.

Getting Out of Town

SOONER OR LATER the time comes when every investigator needs to get out of town. Whether investigating a case, conducting research, escaping local authorities, or simply in need of a vacation, the options are many. A vast rail system links the country, now rivalled by a rapidly expanding long-distance bus industry. The popularity of the personal automobile has led to a federally-funded highway system that spans the width and breadth of America. The fledgling aviation industry, practically non-existent at the end of the War, by the end of the decade has become the most promising form of future transport. The following sections discuss commonly available forms of transportation on land, at sea, and in the air.

Inter-Urban Trolleys

Although only a minor form of commercial transportation, this system deserves mention. An extension of city systems, these electrically powered light rail trains are most common in the East. Linking major cities at central terminals, they allow a passenger to transfer from one to another, touring up and down the East Coast, and as far inland as Cleveland or Detroit. The inter-urbans generally run 24 hours a day, seven days a week. Expanding bus lines have rendered this form of transportation nearly obsolete and by the end of the decade many lines are discontinued.

The inter-urbans are smooth, quiet, and feature scenic routes along the coast and Great Lakes. With good connections a traveler can often make as many as 250 miles a day. Rates vary, but the average cost of travel is approximately 6 cents a mile.

Bus Lines

Research into the development of larger frame vehicles during the War resulted in designs that allow for the safe and transport of large numbers of passengers. A rapidly improving highway system has made commercial long-distance bus service a viable alternative to rail. By 1926 there are bus lines linking all major cities, and by 1928 through service from New York to San Francisco, fresh drivers taking the wheel every six to eight hours. Greyhound is already emerging as a major force in the industry.

Early in the decade bus travel is bumpy, often crowded, and decidedly less pleasant than rail travel. By the end of the decade the bus lines have responded with larger, more comfortable coaches featuring curtained windows, reclining seats, and onboard toilet facilities. The observation bus, developed in California, features a raised passenger section offering unobstructed views while allowing for extra cargo space beneath.

Slower than either rail or the inter-urbans, bus lines offer markedly cheaper rates as well as service to many areas not accessed by rail. The smallest cities usually feature a bus terminal, or at least an official stop in front of a downtown restaurant or hotel. Despite improvements bus travel is still less reliable than rail, suffering more frequently from mechanical breakdowns, accidents, and bad weather conditions.

Fares

Short route bus travel between population centers averages about 20-25 mph and costs roughly 4 cents a mile. Long-distance travel averages 250-300 miles a day and cost about 4 cents a mile. Through buses on long-distance express routes make as many as 750-800 miles a day, cost 6 cents a mile.

Rail Travel

ALTHOUGH SUFFERING FROM government control and increasingly stiff competition from the bus lines, the U.S. rail system is still operating at or near its peak. With nearly a quarter-million miles of rail, U.S. rail companies operate nearly half the world's total rail mileage. The steam locomotive is king, and seems likely to remain so. A few electric locomotives are in operation, and some light-duty oil-electric models do service in rail yards, but experiments with both diesel-compressed air and diesel-electric locomotives have so far shown little promise.

Although freight mileage improves slightly over the decade, passenger mileage drops by more than 30%. Still the fastest, safest, and surest way to travel, the railroads have responded to the decrease in business by improving the quality of their equipment and service, hoping to attract customers.

Passenger Trains

Pullman coaches are the most popular type of passenger coach in America, comprising nearly one-quarter of all the passenger rolling stock in the country. Featuring fold-up berths, Pullmans are offered in wide variety, with differing combinations of sleeping berths and sealed compartments. The latest Pullman model, the "Overnight Car" features 14 individual rooms, each with fold-down bed and private toilet. The Pullman company also owns and operates 21 special 'business coaches' that may be leased by corporations or individuals. These feature beds, private dining facilities, desks, and other amenities as required.

Aside from the Pullman cars, a long-distance passenger train might also include an Observation Car with open compartments and a rear, open-air deck with chairs, Club Cars with card tables, reading material, and attendants, and dining, buffet, and cafe cars.

Fares

The cost of rail travel varies, depending on the wants and needs of the individual. Commuter hops of two hours or less feature little more than a fairly comfortable seat and access to a snack bar. Running between major urban centers and to outlying areas, cost is about 4 cents a mile. Average speed, with frequent stops, is about 20-25 mph.

Longer journeys, regular runs of less than fifteen hours, usually feature dining coaches and club cars. Cost is about 5 cents a mile for tourist accommodations, 7 cents a mile for private, more comfortable, first-class compartments. Frequent stops for mail and freight limit average speeds to about 25-30 mph.

Overnight and longer journeys require Pullman cars along with the necessary attendants, conductors, and porters, all increasing the cost. Stops are infrequent and a fast 'Special' can make from 850-1100 miles a day, traveling from New York to San Francisco in just three days. Rates vary depending upon the type of accommodations desired: 6 cents a mile for a simple Pullman; 8 cents a mile for a small private compartment for two; and 10 cents a mile or more for a First-Class room with private toilet, a car porter and other luxuries. Pullman will lease one of their private cars for $1.50 per mile, with a minimum charge of $75.00 a day. Porters are extra.

A few very rich individuals own their own private rail cars. A standard 70-foot Pullman coach can be purchased for $27,000-$33,000. Custom outfitting and furnishings are, of course, additional. Hauling by train costs $1 per mile.

Freight Shipments

Equipment can also be transported. Regular freight costs about 10 cents per hundred pounds, per hundred miles. A motorcycle costs about 60 cents per hundred miles, an automobile $2.50 to $5 per hundred miles, a loaded coffin about 70 cents per hundred miles. Freight moves at an average of 200-250 miles per day. Express service is available—fast but expensive. Rates are double normal freight, or a little more, but delivery time is much shorter, express freight traveling at up to 1000 miles per day (not including handling time). Investigators traveling a cross-country passenger route and hauling equipment beyond the normal luggage limits may be charged express rates for additional freight.

Automobiles & Others

THE PERSONAL AUTOMOBILE has changed the face of America. By 1929 there are 23,121,000 automobiles on American roads, 612,000 in New York City alone. The U.S. currently manufactures 85% of all automobiles produced in the world, and owns 75% of the world's vehicles. By 1918 New York has erected its first traffic light and by the end of the 1920s One-Way streets, No Left Turns, and No Parking zones are the norm. City streets are resurfaced in macadam and compounds, pure asphalt limited to use in the wealthier neighborhoods where a quiet road surface is considered important. The use of concrete, particularly on main thoroughfares, is showing good results.

When Henry Ford first designed his original Model T he intended a practical design that would serve society forever. By the 1920s, however, the "Tin Lizzie" has been hopelessly outclassed by stylish, powerful vehicles with a wide range of options. Closed cars, once the rarity, now account for 80% of all sales, and by mid-decade exotic colors such as Arabian Sand and Versailles Violet are available. Although fluid-driven, automatic transmissions still lie in the future, modern automobiles feature hydraulic brakes, electric starters, cigarette lighters, and tachometers.

Although Henry Ford prefers to stick with just a single design—the 'T,' then the 'A'—most auto companies have begun the practice of announcing new models every year, premiering them in the fall accompanied by much fanfare.

Although a few electric and steam-powered cars are still produced in small numbers, there is no doubt that gasoline engines have proven themselves superior.

Driving in America

At the beginning of the decade speed limits are generally low. Typically, Illinois set limits of 15 mph in residential areas, 10 mph in built-up areas, and 6 mph on curves. On country roads limits were generally 20 mph, though New

York and California allowed 30. By 1931 top speed limits are generally 35 to 40 mph.

Auto Touring

The rapidly-growing popularity of the automobile urged the federal government to organize an interstate highway system. Seventeen through routes now span the country, comprising over 96,000 miles of improved roads. By 1924 over 31,000 miles is already paved with concrete, the rest at least graded and drained, if not paved with macadam. By the end of the decade, nearly 80% of the system is complete. Routes are marked by numbered shields: a standardized system of warning and information signs that is already being adopted by several states. The system claims that 90% of the U.S. population is now within ten miles of a federal highway.

Regardless, this still leaves nearly three million miles of roads in the hands of state and county agencies. The quality and condition of these roads varies depending on local finances and the amount of use the road receives. Major thoroughfares are surfaced with macadam or other compounds. Major rural roads are graded and reasonably drained. Many roads are sorely neglected.

Average touring speed (with stops) is about 15 mph, although this could be increased to as much as 20 mph if the route confines itself to well-maintained and paved roads. Driving more than eight hours is fatiguing. Without rest, an investigator's Drive Automobile skill begins to suffer.

Auto touring is the American way. Over fifteen million vehicles visit our national forests in 1926; by comparison, less than two million people visit by other means. The popularity has given rise to a camping equipment industry, and the 'auto camp.'

Auto Camps

Long-distance auto touring often requires overnight stays. Hotels are often too expensive, and usually inconveniently located in a downtown area near rail and bus lines. Auto camps are found right along the highway, often near city limits (but outside them, where business regulations are less stringent). They offer easy access to the highway, gasoline and other necessities.

First appearing around 1910, auto camps were originally no more than marked off areas of ground with room for a tent and automobile. Later, small sheds replaced open ground. At 50 cents a night per head, auto tourers were expected to provide their own lights, stove, furniture, etc. After 1925 most auto camp cabins charged $1 a night per person, a fee that includes an iron bed with straw mattress, benches, running water, and a gas hot plate. Towels, sheets, and blankets are available at additional cost. By the mid-20s over 5000 of these establishments are found across the country.

Auto camps soon gained a seedy reputation. Usually located on the outskirts of a city, they often become havens for bootleggers, gypsies, and prostitutes. Add to this the rumor that some camps rent "by the hour" and their reputation is further sullied. In the 1930s, FBI Director J. Edgar Hoover publicly calls for the closing of all auto camps, an unsuccessful campaign.

Licensing

Automobiles must be registered in the state of the investigator's residence. A metal license plate is issued at the time of registration. Operators must have a valid driver's license, also issued by the state.

Choosing an Automobile

ALTHOUGH GASOLINE POWERED cars are the standard, a few steam and electric-powered vehicles are still available. Stanley, producer of the famous 'Stanley Steamer' doesn't go bankrupt until 1927, and the Milburn Electric car, although silent and clean, has a limited cruising range of about thirty miles, and a top speed limited to 40 mph.

New car prices in the late 1920s range from $280 for one of the last Ford Model T's, to $10,000 or more for luxury and performance vehicles. Manufacturers have already created a network of franchised dealerships and the market is competitive. Prices can be bargained. Most dealerships in large cities handle only one make of automobile, but smaller communities with less potential business often combine dealerships, though seldom marketing direct competitors. A combination Ford and Cadillac dealership might be found in a small town like Arkham, Massachusetts. Imported vehicles can sometimes be ordered through a U.S. importer, but these outlets are far

Automobile Perfomance

HIGHER HORSEPOWER means greater top speed and better acceleration. Heavier cars will accelerate slower than lighter models with similar engines, but weight has little effect on top speed. Even the lowest-powered cars are capable of reaching speeds in excess of forty mph. A horsepower of between twenty and thirty usually yields top speeds in the fifty to sixty mph range. Horsepowers of up to 100 allow top speeds up to and including seventy to eighty mph. A 150 hp Rolls-Royce could do ninety-five, a 170 hp Mercedes 116 mph, and the 265 hp Dusenberg claimed a top speed of 118 mph. The world auto speed record, set in 1927, is 231.362 mph.

Model T Roadster

and few between and may require a visit to the nearest large city. Dealerships also provide warranty maintenance as well as regular mechanical repairs. Used cars are plentiful and available but, with little regulation, it is the heyday of the shady used car salesman. *Caveat emptor.*

A few selected models are described in detail below, followed by a list of others, both American and imports.

Ford Model T

The "Tin Lizzie" was conceived by Henry Ford as a car that would never become obsolete. A simple and efficient vehicle, the basic design was continually updated, owners installing their own upgrades as they choose. During a production run from 1908-1927 over fifteen million were produced.

The Model T was an 'everyman's car,' capable of carrying as many as six passengers. Possessed of excellent handling (for its day), the car is easily maintained; most repairs can be performed by the amateur mechanic. First priced at $900, the cost eventually dropped below $300 in later years. Aside from the basic vehicle, the Model T can be ordered as a delivery vehicle, ambulance, or cargo carrier. Speedster and Roadster models were also produced.

Auto Combat

COMBAT BETWEEN automobiles usually involves firearms. Aiming a handgun or other weapon from a moving automobile results in a skill reduced by one-half. If firing at another moving target—a pursuing automobile that is dodging and weaving, reduce the skill by one-half again.

Cars offer good protection. Made of heavy steel panels, automobiles can deflect a good many bullets intended for the occupants. In the 1930s lawmen, discouraged to see their .45 caliber Thompsons bouncing harmlessly off the fleeing felons' Ford, switched to the more powerful BAR. Safety glass has not yet been invented and drivers and passengers may be cut by flying glass.

The 'T' sports a four-cylinder engine and manual transmission with two forward speeds and one reverse. Three separate pedals control the transmission brake, the reverse gear and car brake, and the shifting of gears. The throttle is a lever mounted on the steering wheel.

With its sometimes dangerous hand crank and inefficient, speed-dependent lighting system, the 'T' is finally forced out of production in 1927.

First introduced in 1908, price ranged from $900 to as low as $280.

Ford Model A

When unveiled in 1927, over a million people jammed Ford Motor Company headquarters in New York trying to see the new Ford intended to replace the venerable Model T. With four doors, an open top, and a three-speed transmission, the 'A' was a manifest improvement over its predecessor. However, it never gains the fame nor dominates the market like its forebear.

Introduced in 1927, its price tag is $450.

Chevrolet Capitol

Chevrolet is part of General Motors and a direct competitor to Ford. Production figures topped 239,000 in 1927. The Capitol is available in two-door and four-door models and although capable of reaching speeds of up to 50 mph, the early models are equipped with rear brakes only. Four-wheel braking is introduced in 1928.

First introduced in 1927, its price is $695.

Chevrolet International Model AC Truck

Four versions of this widely-used light truck are offered for sale: the Sedan Delivery, the Pickup, the Canopy or Screen, and the Panel version. Standard equipment includes four-wheel brakes and three-speed manual transmission. Optional front and rear bumpers, heater, cigar lighter, and wire wheels can be special ordered. The roadster pickup is fitted with a slip-in pickup box or cargo carrier.

Studebaker Dictator

Studebaker was formerly a carriage maker, now switched to automobiles. The Dictator series was produced in the tens of thousands and available in ten different models ranging from a two-passenger business coupe to a five-passenger Royal Tourer. The Dictator features standard spare tire lock, speedometer, windshield washer, and shock absorbers and is available in closed-top or open versions.

Introduced in 1928, its price ranges from $900 to $1195.

Packard Twin Six

The Twin Six is noted for its superb acceleration and a top speed of 70 mph. Prices begin at $2600 for the two-seat runabout, higher for the five-passenger versions, and topping at $4440 for the seven-seat limousine. Available in closed-top or open models, standard equipment includes a Warner speedometer, a Waltham clock, complete tool kit, and power tire pump.

First introduced in 1916, it costs $2950.

Dusenberg J

A vehicle for the truly discriminating, like all Dusenbergs it was handmade by skilled craftsmen using only the finest materials. The liquid-cooled eight-cylinder engine could power the car to a top speed of 118 mph, accelerating from 0 to 99 mph in twenty-one seconds, despite its great weight. Aside from the usual instrumentation, the Dusenberg could be ordered with an altimeter, barometer, and gauges to monitor tire pressure, oil changes, radiator water level, and brake fluid levels. Coachwork was custom, and often done by craftsmen outside Dusenberg.

Introduced in 1929, a Dusenberg costs $20,000 or more.

Import Specials

Lancia Lambda 214

This Italian-built motor car debuted in 1923 with many features new to the industry. Rather than the common pressed steel chassis, the designers opted for a monocoque hull built up from hollow steel pressings. A four-door, closed-top vehicle, the 214 could reach speeds of 125 mph.

The Lancia is priced at $4050.

Mercedes-Benz SS

The SS is an expensive sport and racing car produced by Daimler-Benz of Stuttgart, Germany. Normally a four-door, open-top car, a specially-produced two-seater has won a number of races in Europe and South America. Carefully hand-crafted, fewer than 300 of the entire series are manufactured by 1934.

Additional Automobiles

THE FOLLOWING IS A mere sampling of the many automobiles produced after the War. Prices are approximate and vary according to options, shipping costs, etc. Seating is also approximate, many models being available in a range of styles from two-seater roadster to seven-passenger limousine. Similarly, many models are also available in both open-top and closed versions. Year indicates the year that model was first introduced. HP is the horsepower of the engine.

Make/Model	Price	Year	Seating	HP
Buick Model C-45	$950	1915	5	22.5
Buick Model D-45	$1020	1916	5	45
Buick Model E-45	$1265	1918	5	65
Buick Master Six Model 40	$1495	1925	5	70
Buick Series 116 Model 27	$1320	1929	5	94
Cadillac Type 55	$2240	1917	4	31.25
Cadillac Type 61	$4690	1922	5	60
Cadillac V-63	$3950	1924	5	80
Cadillac Series 314	$3195	1925	5	80
Cadillac Series 341-B	$3695	1928	5	90
Cadillac Series 452	$6950	1930	5	185
Chevrolet Model M	$695	1923	5	26
Chevrolet Model F	$495	1924	5	26
Chevrolet Model K	$525	1925	5	26
Chevrolet Capitol Model AA	$695	1927	5	26
Chrysler Model F-58	$1045	1926	5	38
Chrysler Model 65	$1075	1929	5	70
Dodge Model 30	$835	1917	5	35
Dodge Model S/1	$985	1922	5	35
Dodge Model DD	$865	1930	5	60
Dusenberg J	$20,000	1929	5	265
Ford Model T	$360	1908	5	22.5
Ford Model A	$450	1927	4	40
Hudson Super Six Series J	$1750	1916	4	76
Hudson Model S	$1175	1927	5	92
Hudson Model R	$1350	1929	5	92
Hudson Model L	$1850	1929	5	92
Ideal Stutz Bearcat	$2000	1912	2	60
Oldsmobile 43-T	$1095	1915	5	30
Oldsmobile 43-AT	$1345	1923	5	40

Make/Model	Price	Year	Seating	HP
Oldsmobile 30-DD4S	$1115	1926	5	41
Packard Twin Six Touring	$2950	1916	7	88
Packard Single Six	$1495	1922	5	54
Packard Standard Eight	$2285	1929	5	90
Pierce-Arrow	$6000	1921	6	110
Pontiac 6-27	$825	1926	5	40
Pontiac 6-28 Sedan	$745	1928	5	25.3
Stanley Steamer Model F	$1500	1907	5	20
Studebaker Lgt 6 Model EJ	$1485	1920	5	40
Studebaker Stnd. 6 Sedan	$1595	1925	5	50
Studebaker Stnd./Dictator	$1165	1927	5	50
Studebaker Dict. Ryl. Tourer	$1195	1928	5	50
LIGHT TRUCKS				
Chevrolet Int. AC Pickup	$545	1929	3	46
Dodge 1/2 ton Model 1919	$1085	1919	3	35
Dodge 3/4 ton Model DC	$895	1927	3	35
Ford Model TT Truck	$490	1923	3	22.5
Ford Model 82 B Pickup	$435	1930	3	40
IMPORTS				
Austin Seven England	$825	1923	4	10.5
Bentley 3-Litre England	$9000	1920	5	65
BMW Dixi Germany	$1225	1928	2	15
Citroen B2 France	$800	1921	2	20
Citroen C3 France	$800	1921	2	11
Hispano-Suiza Alfonso Spain	$4000	1912	2	65
Lancia Lambda 214 Italy	$4050	1923	6	49
Mercedes-Benz SS Germany	$7750	1928	4	170
Renault AX France	$500	1909	2	14
ROLLS-ROYCE England				
Silver Ghost	$6750	1907	6	48
Phantom I	$10,800	1925	6	100

First appearing in 1928, the Mercedes has a price tag of $7750.

Rolls-Royce Model 40/50 Silver Ghost

Rolls-Royce features autos manufactured individually, rather than mass-produced. The Silver Ghost, fast for it time, is also noted for its exceptional quiet and comfort. Only the chassis and power trains are made by Rolls-Royce; the bodies are built to specification by various coachmakers in England and the U.S.

From 1907-1925, 6,173 Silver Ghosts were produced with an average price tag of $6750.

Auto Accessories

The popularity of the automobile has spawned a burgeoning industry supplying replacement and custom parts. A few examples follow: wool car blanket, $1.98-$11.50; car cover, $6.45; Spanish-trim seat covers, $9.95; stripe window awnings, $1.69 a pair; tires, $5.65-$13.45 each; spoked steel wheel, $4.00; battery, $8.35-$14.95; nickel-plated winged radiator cap, 65 cents; fan belt, 24 cents; lighted turn-signal system, $2.98 (not installed); locking steering wheel, $8.95; spark plug, 25 cents; floor mats, $1.49-$3.10; window shades, $1.55; cut-glass hanging flower vase, $1.15; pickup bed for Ford or Chevrolet roadster, $7.75-$8.95; 1-gallon emergency gas can, 78 cents; tire chains, $3.95 a pair; auto first-aid kit, $2.57; smokeless charcoal heater, $2.45; electric engine warmer, $2.25; dash-mounted oil level gauge, $1.25; Simoniz car wax, 44 cents a can; polishing mitt, 35 cents; folding running-board luggage carrier, $1.25.

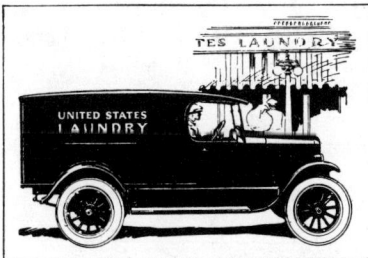

Trucks & Buses

LARGER VEHICLES MAY be required to transport heavy equipment or personnel to an investigation site. Design improvements made during the War have resulted in larger and more manageable trucks. Most are equipped with power brakes, and experiments with power steering systems promise that even larger designs will soon hit the road. Aside from typical open or closed cargo trucks, flatbeds and tanker styles are also available. Prices range from $500 or less for a small truck, to $6000 and more for a tractor and trailer.

Buses capable of hauling as many forty people are available. They are equipped with air brakes and special, electrical transmissions. Cost is $2500 to $3500.

Motorcycles

MOTORCYCLES ARE AN exciting option for the young and reckless. Although generally less reliable than automobiles, requiring more maintenance, and unsuitable during inclement weather, they are affordable, quick and maneuverable—and not necessarily bound to travel on established roads. Top speeds on the larger models are comparable or superior to most automobiles and the standing-start acceleration of even smaller models can't be touched. Under good conditions they handle turns faster than automobiles, although this advantage quickly disappears in the presence of rain, snow, ice or mud. Deceleration from medium and slow speeds is superior to most automobiles due to the motorcycle's reduced mass, however, braking systems on many production motorcycles are notoriously inefficient at high speeds, the usual single rear brake quickly overheating and fading into nothingness. Front suspensions are of differing designs of various efficiencies; rear suspensions are non-existent on American motorcycles, resulting in a 'hardtail' design and a bone-jarring ride. The world top speed record for motorcycles in 1927 is 121 mph—with sidecar, 110 mph.

It was not until the War that motorcycle design and engineering received the attention it deserved. The perfection of chain drive systems and reliable counter-shaft transmissions have helped make this vehicle a viable form of transportation. Traditionally used by the military and courier services, the mounted motorcycle policeman is today a common sight in American cities and on highways. The powerful large-displacement Indians and Har-

Motorcycle Performance Figures

SPECIFICATIONS FOR American motorcycles are as follows: Light motorcycles are single-cylinder designs approximately 21 cubic inches (350 cc). They develop around 10-12 hp, hit top speeds of 55 mph, and get 80-100 miles to a gallon of gasoline. Medium motorcycles are 37-45 cubic inches (600-750 cc), have 16 hp, top speeds of 70 mph, and get 60-80 miles to the gallon. Heavy motorcycles of 61-74 cubic inches weigh in excess of 500 lbs., hit top speeds of 100 mph and more, and get 40-60 miles to the gallon.

ley-Davidsons are a choice of police departments across the nation, and around the world.

Motorcycles require frequent maintenance, more so than most automobiles, even including adjustments to fuel and lubrication while riding. Total-loss oil systems and manual spark retards mean an investigator using a motorcycle for regular transportation should have a Mechanical Repair skill of no less than 35%, or suffer the risk of being occasionally stranded with a broken chain, wet magneto, or other routine problem. It should be noted that although most medium and large-displacement motorcycles are powered by four-cycle engines, a few smaller models use the two-cycle engine design. Although simpler, with fewer moving parts, two-cycle engines require their own special maintenance, not the least of which requires mixing lubricating oil with the gasoline. Failure to do so results in a ruined engine.

Passengers

Most motorcycles have room for a passenger to be carried on a pillion seat mounted behind the rider's saddle. Detachable and permanent sidecars, large enough to carry one or two passengers, or a few hundred pounds of equipment can be purchased for $24.95 to $66.95. The military has experimented with mounting light and medium machine guns on sidecars, fired by the passenger. The added weight of sidecar and passenger drastically reduce acceleration and deceleration, and radically affect handling. No longer able to lean into a turn, the motorcycle must be slowed and turned, more in the manner of an automobile.

Licensing

Motorcycles must be registered as a vehicle and bear a license plate. A valid driver's license is required to legally operate a motorcycle on any public street or highway.

American Brand Motorcycles

Numerous makes of American motorcycles have come and gone, leaving four major manufacturers currently dominating the market: Cleveland, Excelsior, Harley-

Davidson, and Indian. Much smaller than the auto companies, a customer, for a price, can request custom designs, alterations, and even high-powered production racers. In America, larger displacement models are designated by a number such as 55 or 74, indicating the cubic-inch displacement of the engine. 74 cubic inches is roughly equal to 1200 cc (cubic centimeters) 45 equal to 750 cc, etc. (Note that British motorcycles of this era are often rated by 'horsepower,' an arbitrary number derived from the displacement of the engine and in no way reflecting the actual output of the motor. 100 cc is equal to 1 horsepower, hence a 10 hp engine is actually a 1000 cc engine that may have more or less than 10 horsepower.) Three-speed transmissions are standard on most American production motorcycles. Prices range from $125 for small, lightweight machines, to $500 and more for a 74-inch stroker. Special machines such as production racers, imports, and foreign luxury machines may cost even more. American designs favor large engines that can effortlessly cruise at high speeds over the highway system. They are also quite heavy, the result of heavy-duty frames and suspension systems that take into account the vast number of unimproved roads in this country.

Cleveland—Cleveland, Ohio

Also a maker of automobiles, this manufacturer has long specialized in smaller, single-cylinder two-stroke motorcycles. In 1929 they introduce a large displacement four in-line, four-stroke touring machine but, nonetheless, go out of business in the early 1930s.

Excelsior—Chicago, Illinois

Excelsior specializes in larger displacement four-strokes, including the 'Super X' 45-inch and 'Series 20' 61-inch, both powerful V-Twins. The latter, first introduced in 1919, features a brass headlight powered by a separate acetylene tank. Charles Lindbergh is the proud owner of a 1919 model Series 20 Excelsior.

Harley-Davidson—Milwaukee, Wisconsin

Harley-Davidson produces a wide range of models including a 37 cubic-inch opposed twin, and 45, 55, 61, and 74 cubic-inch V-twins. They have sold thousands of units to both the military and police forces, exporting large shipments to countries as far away as China and South America.

Indian—Springfield, Massachusetts

Indian is H-D's major competitor, often excelling the latter's sales to the military and police. The most popular Indian, the Scout, is a 36-inch V-Twin. The Chief measures 45 inches, and The Big Chief, a full 74-incher, produces 24 hp and has a top speed well over 110 mph. Late this decade, Indian introduces a four-cylinder in-line touring machine.

Imported Motorcycles

There are many foreign makes of motorcycles, although importers and distributors in the U.S. are rare. Investigators may have to make their own sales and shipping arrangements, including customs, etc. Difficulties in obtaining replacement parts sometimes makes ownership impractical.

Echoing the differences in bicycle designs, American motorcycle manufacturers favor large-displacement touring machines suited for both highways and back roads. European designs tend toward small and medium-displacement machines intended for narrow, twisting roads that are mostly paved. A well developed racing circuit has also helped lead to advanced suspension systems, overhead valve and cam designs, and multi-speed gearboxes.

Germany produces the famed BMW, Austria the Puch, while France, Italy, Belgium, Switzerland, and Sweden all manufacture their own designs. The world's leading manufacturer of motorcycles is Great Britain, producing 120,000 units in 1927 compared to 60,000 for the Germans, and 45,000 for America. English brands include Royal Enfield, B.S.A., Norton, Vellocette, Villiers, and the near-legendary Brough Superior, chosen mount of Colonel T.E. Lawrence of Desert Revolt fame.

Motorcycle Accessories

Goggles ($2.49), padded leather helmets ($4.89), and kidney belts ($1.98) are recommended for both rider and passenger. Leather saddlebags can be mounted over the rear fender, and extra lights, as well as gauges and meters can also be installed. Tall leather boots, and heavy padded clothing helps prevent injury in the case of a spill.

Boats & Others

ALTHOUGH WATER TRAVEL is not the most common way of getting about, the topic bears coverage. The U.S. has several thousand miles of navigable coastline along its eastern, southern, and western borders. Patrolled by the Coast Guard, and marked by buoys and lighthouses, this can be a pleasant, if not particularly fast method of travel. The Great Lakes of the Midwest are large enough, and dangerous enough, to challenge any sailor, and much of the rest of the country is dotted with lakes and marked by navigable rivers.

Small Craft

For purposes of description, small craft are those boats that can be transported either atop an automobile, or on a very light trailer. Most are suitable only for inland lakes and bays, or in calm coastal waters.

Skill—Sailing

THE BASIC Sailing skill applies only to small, one-sail craft. Large craft with more than one sail or mast call for Large Craft Sailing skill which can only be obtained by practicing the Small Craft Sailing skill. Any character with a Small Craft Sailing skill of 50% or more qualifies for a basic Large Craft Sailing skill of 20%, the minimum required to safely maneuver such a vessel. By extension, Large Craft Sailing, practiced until the skill reaches or exceeds 50%, qualifies a character to handle a larger, full-sized sailing ship, investing him with a basic starting Ship Sailing skill of 20%—if, of course, such a vessel can ever be found.

Folding Boats

Folding boats, made of canvas with wooden frames, cost $29.95 or more. They are not particularly strong, nor seaworthy, but with a total weight of less than thirty pounds (which can be divided among bearers) and of unobtrusive size when folded, they are particularly useful when space and weight are prime considerations—underground explorations, etc. Usually rowed or paddled, some can be fitted with a small outboard motor.

Canoes

Wooden canoes are light and relatively inexpensive, costing anywhere from $35 on up, plus $2 each for paddles. Generally fifteen to eighteen feet in length, they can be paddled or portaged overland by one man. Managing a canoe requires a separate Canoe skill with a base chance of 20%. Novices can best learn basic canoe skills by paddling the front seat of a two-man canoe, allowing an experienced canoeist to sit in the rear, steering and maneuvering.

Canoes are notoriously tipsy and care must be taken to avoid capsizing. Items stowed in a canoe should be lashed down and waterproofed as well as possible.

Rowboats

Rowboats, usually clinker built, are comparatively large and heavy, less maneuverable, but more stable than canoes, especially when loaded. Small rowboats can easily carry four to five adults, even more in a pinch. Powered by oars, it takes no particular skill to maneuver a rowboat. Rowboats are particularly adaptable to outboard motor use.

A new rowboat can be had for as little as $35, plus $2.50 each for oars.

Outboard Designs

Particularly favored in America, the original outboard motor was designed in 1910 by Ole Evinrude of Milwaukee, Wisconsin. Quickly mounted or detached, outboard motors offer a flexibility and ease of repair unheard of with inboard designs.

Small, two-cycle outboard motors come in more or less standard sizes of 2, 4, and 8 hp. The smallest weighs fifty pounds and can propel a small rowboat to a speed of 6-8 mph. The price is just $97.50. The two larger models ($189.50, and $279.50) are recommended for mounting only on specially designed craft.

Eight to sixteen feet long, hydroplanes specifically designed for outboards can reach speeds of almost 30 mph with an 8 hp engine. V-shaped displacement hulls, more stable in rough water, cut top speeds drastically, but still make almost 20 mph. Late in the decade, outboards of up to 35 hp become available and in 1929 an outboard-powered craft sets a record of 41.7 mph. Outboard designs are simple and relatively cheap, costing about $25 per foot; the motor is, of course, a separate expense.

Despite the advantages of cheaper cost, more speed, and ease of maintenance, outboards are more suited for lakes and calm waters. Rough seas or surf can easily swamp an outboard, flooding the carburetor and shorting out the electrical system.

Sailboats

Sailboats are still useful, but probably less so in this age of powered craft. Sailing a small vessel with a single sail requires a special Sailing Skill (small craft). An hour or two of lessons give most investigators a basic skill of 20%, enough to insure that they can get around on a smooth lake or bay, but not necessarily enough to make a difficult series of tacks back to shore.

A sailboat can be no more than a rowboat fitted with mast, sail, and rudder, but a dory or other authentic sailing craft costs in the neighborhood of $40 per foot, complete with sails and rigging. Many can be fitted with auxiliary outboard motors.

Large Craft

Large craft are boats that usually remain moored at docks. They can be cartaged overland but require special heavy-duty trailers and trucks. Powered large craft operate much like automobiles and are usually fitted with steering wheels, electric starters, and other familiar controls. Investigators usually have an automatic Pilot Boat skill of 20%. Yachts are large sailing craft and require a special Sailing skill to operate. Note that although larger ships are built of steel, and Germany is presently experimenting with an alloy called Duralumin, all boats, large and small, are currently made of wood.

Open Launches

Powered by one or more inboard engines, open launches are generally high-speed craft. Taking advantage of hydroplane design, they are used for patrol and rescue operations, and by bootleggers and smugglers as well. Generally 16-35 feet long, they are equipped with engines providing 6-30 hp and can usually reach speeds of 25-35 knots (30-40 mph)—and some as high as 55 knots (63 mph).

Launches are not intended for extended periods at sea. Powerful engines devour fuel at a frightful rate and the high-speed hydroplane design is at a disadvantage in rough waters. Canvas covers can be mounted to protect crew and passengers from sun and rain. Cost is generally $75 per foot.

Cabin Cruisers

Cabin Cruisers are intended for extended traveling. V-shaped displacement hulls are more stable in rough seas and lower-powered engines consume less fuel, increasing cruising ranges. Usually 20 feet or longer, cruisers are powered by 10-20 hp engines and have top speeds of 8-10 knots (9-11 mph). American style 'Express' cruisers are 25-50 feet long and, taking advantage of increased fuel capacity, use high-powered engines to reach speeds of 20-25 knots (22-30 mph).

In addition, cabin cruisers are fitted with below decks cabins, galleys, and heads. A 25-foot cruiser can easily sleep six, more if conditions allow sleeping on deck. Cabin cruisers are considerably more expensive than simple open launches, costing about $125 dollars per foot.

Yachts

Yachts are defined as any large craft powered primarily by sails. They may be fitted with one, two, or more masts. Sailing craft are much more delicate and finely tuned vessels, relying on their shape and design, rather than the brute horsepower of internal combustion engines. They are costlier to build, and require a delicate hand to manage.

A minimum Sailing skill (large craft) of 20% is required to properly handle a yacht. This cannot be obtained until an individual has practiced and improved his Small Craft Sailing skill to the point where it reaches or exceeds 50%. The handling of multiple sails, masts, rudder, and balky crew, calls for far more skill than coasting a dory. Note that it is becoming more and more common to fit yachts with small auxiliary engines for use in emergencies and in harbors. They are rarely powerful enough to make more than 4-6 knots (5-7 mph), but under power a yacht can be maneuvered using a Pilot Boat skill.

The best American yachts come from New England shipyards, particularly around Essex, and are constructed by families long in the trade. A custom made yacht, with all sails and rigging, costs $200 to $250 a foot—or more—depending on the materials and fittings.

Boating Accessories

Cork life rings cost $2.50 each; personal life belts, $2.39, the bulkier but safer life jacket, $3.29. Boat hooks cost $4.89. Charts of local waters may be obtained at minimal price. Binoculars are recommended, as are emergency lights if the possibility of being caught in darkness exists. A flare gun, just in case, costs $24.95. A line throwing gun, appearing something like a carbine, fires a 3/16-inch line up to 60 yards, and costs $55. A larger version, the Lyle gun, is a brass, 18-inch cannon that can hurl an 18 lb. rod and half-inch line up to 700 yards, costing $300. The Sven Foyn harpoon gun fires an explosive harpoon 30-40 yards. It costs $895.

Receiving radios suitable for maritime application become commercially available near the end of the decade. Costing $250 and more, they allow boaters to monitor weather and Coast Guard reports. Two-way radios that allow the boaters to transmit back lie in the future.

And just in case: steel fishing rod, $3.98; best bamboo rod, $12.95; reels, $2.69 to $22.50; lures, 19 cents to $1.10; tackle box, $5.98; preserved minnows, 24 cents a jar.

Air Travel

FOLLOWING THE END of the War the U.S. aviation industry was small, unsupported, and nearly stagnant. Airplanes were viewed as sporting devices and there was no federal regulation or pilot's licensing required until the Air Commerce Act of 1926. Until this time pilots were only required to obey the laws of their state and local community, most regulations dealing with the buzzing of towns and farms, and other reckless stunts.

Early Air Mail

In 1920 the U.S. Postal Service inaugurated their New York to San Francisco, cross-country air mail service. Air mail had, since the end of the War, flown regularly between New York and Washington D.C., but nothing of this scale had yet been attempted. Using Curtiss and other Army surplus planes, ex-military pilots flying in shifts crossed the country in just 32 hours, compared to three days for the fastest trains. Although at first uneconomical, within a few years a profit was shown. Night flying began in 1924 when the route between Chicago and Rock Springs, Wyoming, was completely lighted. By 1926, when the Postal Service got out of the business, selling its routes to private contractors, lighted airways stretched all the way from New York to the Rocky Mountains. By the end of the decade the U.S. has over 15,000 miles of marked airways.

Aside from mail and passenger transport, aircraft are currently being used for aerial survey and photography,

Curtiss JN-4 "Flying Jenny"

forest fire reconnaissance, crop-dusting, sky-writing, and are occasionally pressed into ambulance and medical service.

The U.S. Airway System

The U.S. airway system consists of sixty-six major airfields, located roughly 250 miles apart, each lit by two floodlights of a half-billion candlepower each, one lighting the field while the other sweeps the horizon every twenty seconds—a beacon seen for 100 miles or more. Small emergency fields are located every 15-30 miles, lit by smaller electric beacons. Small acetylene beacons are placed every three miles along the routes to help guide pilots. Looking from New York, two major lighted routes are seen: one heading south down the coast to Washington, D.C., before turning inland to Atlanta, Georgia, then branching west to Birmingham, Alabama, and south to Daytona Beach, Florida. The other heads due west to Cleveland, Detroit, then Chicago which forms a 'hub' for short routes to many Midwestern cities. West of Chicago a light route heads to Omaha, here branching south to Dallas, Texas (and an unlighted portion all the way to Houston), and west to Cheyenne, Wyoming, and over the Rocky Mountains to Salt Lake City, Utah. From Salt Lake City routes head northwest to Portland, west to San Francisco, and southwest to Los Angeles. A completely lighted route also runs the length of the West Coast.

Use of the Airways

The airways are for the use of commercial companies and private citizens alike. The 66 major airfields linking the system offer hangars, repairs, fuel, wireless and meteorological equipment, booking offices for commercial carriers, and even travel agents. A Take-Off and Landing fee of $2 is charged. Gasoline sells for roughly 19 cents a gallon.

Normal cruising altitude is around 5000 feet, although heights of 10,000 feet can be safely reached without resorting to oxygen. At 12,000-15,000 feet the effects of oxygen deprivation can be felt, and pilots and passengers may be at risk. Fully pressurized cabins do not appear until the next decade.

Commercial Air Travel

After establishing the system, the U.S. Post Office sold its air mail routes to 32 private contractors who now haul not only mail, but express freight and passengers as well. In addition to the normal mail routes, commercial companies have established a number of other routes, particularly across the South and Southwest. None of these routes are lighted, however.

Air travel is not prohibitively expensive: 10 cents a mile is about the average rate, and speeds average about 100 mph, including refueling time. In 1929, "Lindbergh's line" offers the first through cross-country package. Passenger flying is not yet done at night, and in the evening the passengers are set down and transported by bus to make rail connections. Traveling by rail overnight, the passengers the following morning disembark and are transported to the nearest airfield. Price is $335 one way.

Air Taxis

Air-Taxi service is also available. Private pilots with their own aircraft often offer charter aircraft service to destinations not on regular commercial routes. Rates are generally 25 cents a mile for a medium sized plane capable of carrying three investigators in addition to the pilot.

The selling off of the Postal Service air mail routes gives rise to new companies like National Air Transport and Boeing Air Transport. Mergers later create companies called TWA, Eastern Airlines, and American Airlines. Although amenities such as stewards, on-board lavatories, seat belts, and in-flight meals are not intro-

The Air Commerce Act of 1926

UNTIL THIS DATE there is no uniform regulation of aircraft or air traffic. With the assumption of the air mail routes by private carriers numerous laws and regulations were instituted. Pilot's licenses became required, and individuals were certified as flying instructors. Aircraft inspections and insurance become mandatory, and airfields required to meet certain minimum standards. Airfields must be clearly marked, landing strips graded and drained, and wind direction indicators installed. To receive an 'A' rating, an airfield must be equipped with lights, have runways at least 2500 feet long, and allow take-offs and landings in at least eight directions. Ratings go as low as 'F' or 'X' (unrated). By late 1928 there are over 4000 rated airfields in operation.

Typical Early Airlines

The immediate years following the Great War showed only limited advancement in the area of commercial air transport. Cramped, noisy, uncomfortable conditions in early aircraft made their advantage of slightly decreased travel time fade when compared with the relative luxury of a passenger train's Pullman car. Aeromarine Airways was one of the first U.S airlines to show any sign of success. Operating from 1919 till 1923, Aeromarine offered passenger service from New York to Atlantic City, New Jersey, later moving south and flying routes between Miami and Nassau helping to quench the thirsts of drinkers escaping Prohibition restrictions. Using Curtiss seaplanes purchased from the U.S. Navy for $6000-$9000 each, Aeromarine soon expanded

their routes to Havana. Before folding in 1923 regular or special flights linked a string of cities from Detroit, to Cleveland, and all the way to Cuba.

It was not until the mid-1920s that commercial airlines became a viable interest and in 1925 Ryan Airlines was founded, the first truly successful airline. Starting with a handful of converted war surplus biplanes, Ryan was the first to offer year-round service. Its first San Diego to Los Angeles route cost $17.50 one-way, $26.50 round-trip, including ground transportation to and from the airfield. The airline carried some 5600 passengers in 1926 but closed the following year when owner T. Claude Ryan chose to concentrate instead on aircraft manufacture. Lindbergh's "Spirit of St. Louis" was a Ryan monoplane.

duced until the thirties, the traveler who does not mind the noise, cold, and general risk, will find small airlines often the quickest way to get from one place to another.

Private Aircraft

A PRIVATELY OWNED AIRPLANE might be thought a luxury, but it is really not out of reach of the typical investigator's wallet. War surplus trainers can be had for as little as $300. Hangar fees, fuel, maintenance, and takeoff and landing fees add only a little to the total cost.

The decade sees great advances in design. At the end of the War most airplanes are simple open-cockpit biplanes constructed of wood, wire, and silk. By 1930 fully enclosed, multi-engine monoplanes capable of carrying 10 or more people hundreds of miles non-stop in relative comfort are being constructed wholly of metal. However, U.S. aircraft production lags far behind many European countries. In 1928 America produced only 5000 planes, nearly half of these inexpensive, open-cockpit biplanes. Of the remainder, a mere eighty-five were advanced design closed-cockpit monoplanes, and only sixty were of transport size.

A typical airplane is capable of cruising at speeds from 70-100 mph, with a range of 250-400 miles. But airplanes can be customized to suit the user's needs. Larger, more powerful engines can be fitted to increase speed, and additional fuel tanks installed to improve cruising range. Aircraft powerplants are expensive, however, and newer, more powerful models typically cost thousands of dollars. The weight of additional fuel means less passenger and/or cargo capacity, and may also drastically alter the flight characteristics of the aircraft. All these must be taken into account when making modifications.

Seaplanes

Seaplanes and flying boats get particular attention from designers. Because they can take-off and land on water, they are not limited by normal-length landing strips. Seaplanes are among the largest and most powerful aircraft available.

Float type seaplanes appear as typical small or medium aircraft (up to 10,000 pounds) fitted with pontoons instead of wheels. These floats decrease both cargo capacity and top speed by 10%. A world speed record of 281.669 mph is set in October, 1927, by a British-built seaplane.

Flying boats are larger aircraft whose hulls ride directly in the water. One of the largest weighs over 33,000 pounds, has a crew of five, and is powered by four engines developing over 2600 hp. Reasonably seaworthy, flying boats can set down in bad weather to ride out the storm, then take off again.

Instrumentation

Although new instruments and indicators are constantly being developed, the typical cockpit includes: a tachometer; engine oil and temperature gauges; an Air Speed indicator; an Altimeter; Attitude or Trim indicators; possibly Climb and Bank indicators; and perhaps a two-way radio.

Common Aircraft

The following are just a few representative models of aircraft available. Some are manufactured strictly for the commercial market while others are civilian models of aircraft originally designed for the military. Some, especially trainers, are actual military surplus.

Setting prices for aircraft is problematical. A small market, coupled with specialized needs, results in many early aircraft designs being built to order. Occasionally some of those manufactured are not delivered for one reason or another, and are eventually sold by the manufacturer for a lower than normal cost. War surplus equipment often affords the buyer remarkable bargains. Used aircraft prices fluctuate wildly, depending on condition and local demand. Exact costs will have to be determined by the keeper. As a rule of thumb, open-cockpit biplanes are the cheapest, monoplanes and closed hatches far more costly. Twin engines usually at least double the price.

Skill—Airplane Navigation

FLYING OVER KNOWN territory with familiar landmarks, or following a marked air route, requires little in the way of navigation. Over unfamiliar territory, or if a marked air route is lost, Airplane Navigation is essential to accurately locate the craft's position.

Airplane navigating is done by a method called Dead Reckoning (D.R.). Involving the use of several unique instruments and methods, it must be taught by an experienced teacher, or learned through study. Using an aero-bearing plate, a wind-gauge bearing plate, and a course-setting sight, the pilot can figure the wind speed, direction of aircraft drift and other factors to arrive at a true position. Navigation by the stars is used only as a back-up method to check the results of dead reckoning.

In the latter part of the decade two-way aircraft radios become available. In an emergency a radio can sometimes be used to locate one's position. Two ground stations monitoring an airplane's distress call can often plot the craft's position. Experiments with radio beacons, monitored by approaching aircraft, show future promise. Navigating by night is not too difficult, particularly when keeping to lighted airways. Fog is the true danger, and pilots, lacking any visual coordinates, find they have to use their instruments just to keep the plane upright and level. Even lighted airfields can be difficult to locate in thick fog.

Avro 504K

Thousands of this two-seater biplane were manufactured between 1916 and 1918, after the war many finding their way into the hands of barnstormers and other performers. The Avro saw service all over the world, including Japan, Australia, Europe, and South America, as well as the U.S. A versatile aircraft, the 504 can be fitted with both ski and float type landing devices, in addition to the normal gear. Military versions carried a single, synchronized machine gun.

The standard factory price in England is approximately (868 pounds) $3900 without engine, $4300 (907 pounds) with a 130 hp Clerget powerplant, slightly cheaper with the 110 hp LeRhone. Civilians could often buy them as cheaply as $2900 (650 pounds)—engine included.

Powered by the Clerget, the Avro can hit a top speed of 95 mph, and has a cruising range of 250 miles.

Curtiss JN-4 "Flying Jenny"

An open-cockpit biplane, the Jenny features tandem seating for two, with dual controls. The result of development of earlier Curtiss designs used in the war against Pancho Villa, the JN-4 biplane is the most common aircraft in the U.S. military during the early part of the decade. Thousands of pilots trained in the Jenny during the War and in years after. A reliable aircraft, it is the first mass-produced aircraft in the U.S. Beginning in 1916 approximately 7,280 are manufactured, 4,800 for the U.S. Army alone. After the War, used Jennys could be purchased for as little as $50-$600, and were the commonly used by barnstormers in their traveling shows.

Powered by a Curtiss engine developing 90 hp, the Jenny has a top speed of 75 mph and a cruising range of 150 miles.

Farman F.60 *Goliath*

First designed in 1919, the French *Goliath* was the first truly commercial airliner. With a crew of two, and seating twelve passengers, this twin-engine biplane began regular air service between Paris and London in 1920 and sports a perfect safety record.

The *Goliath* is powered by twin Salmson engines that develop a combined 520 hp. It can cruise at 75 mph, and has a cruising range of 248 miles.

Felixstowe F.2A

A central hull seaplane designed for maritime patrol and anti-submarine warfare in 1917, the F.2A biplane was responsible for the destruction of several German submarines and a few zeppelins as well. Standard military armament included four to seven Lewis guns, plus racks holding two 230 pound bombs. These aircraft, sans armament, can be picked up for reasonable prices as military surplus. They make effective cargo or passenger carriers.

The F.2A seats six and is powered by twin Rolls-Royce engines developing a combined 690 hp. It has a top speed of 95 mph, and a cruising range of 500 miles.

Sopwith 7F.1 *Snipe*

The successor to the famous Sopwith *Camel*, the *Snipe* biplane fighter first saw service in 1917. After the war it was retained by the RAF and used as a trainer until 1926. Occasionally available as military surplus, its usefulness is limited by its single seat and minimal cargo capacity. Military fighter versions were typically outfitted with a pair of synchronized Vickers machine guns mounted above the engine housing.

Powered by a 230 hp Bentley engine, the *Snipe* has a top speed of 121 mph, and a cruising range of 300 miles.

Junkers F13

This all metal, single-engine monoplane is a design well ahead of its time. Although the cockpit is open, the passenger compartment is enclosed, and well upholstered. Designed specifically for the civilian market, 322 are built between 1919 and 1932, some of them employed by national air forces as cargo carriers. The F13 is the first aircraft of its type to be equipped with safety belts, and can employ wheel, float, or ski-type landing gear.

Seating four, in addition to two crew members, the Junkers is powered by a 185 hp BMW engine. Cruising speed is 87 mph, and cruising range 435 miles.

Dornier Do 15 *Wal*

Production of this aircraft began in 1923 and continues until 1932. The basic design benefits from continual improvements, including upgraded engines as well as changes to wingspan and to overall weight. A flying boat with high-mounted single wing, the *Wal* mounts its twin engines above the high wing in a push-pull configuration. Designed in Germany, the first *Wals* were manufactured in Italy, Germany's production restricted by its postwar agreements. One of the best aircraft of its type, the mili-

Transport & Travel

tary reconnaissance version is armed with a pair of MG15 7.92mm machine guns, and can carry as many as four 110 lb. bombs on external racks.

One of the aircraft's most famous flights was Roald Admundsen's attempt to fly a pair over the North Pole. One plane crashed on pack ice forcing the other to make a tricky landing to retrieve the stranded crew of the wreck. After hacking through the ice to provide a strip of water suitable for take-off, the overloaded *Wal* managed to return the expedition safely home.

Seating four, the *Wal* is powered by a pair of BMW engines developing a combined 1500 hp. The *Wal* can hit a top speed of 137 mph, cruise at 118, and has a range of 1367 miles.

Fokker F.VIIA/3m

A product of the famous Dutch Fokker firm, the F.VII monoplane began life as a single engine utility transport in 1923. In 1925 a trimotor version was introduced that was destined to earn the airplane its greatest successes. Adaptable to skis and floats, the F.VIIA/3m sees service all over the world. Eleven have been purchased by the U.S. Army and designated C-2 cargo carriers.

The aircraft's most famous moment comes on May 9, 1926 when a Fokker F.VII carries Richard Byrd and copilot Floyd Bennett safely over the North Pole. Other records set by this plane include a 2400 mile flight from Oakland, California, to Hawaii, and in 1929 a world endurance record staying aloft for 150.67 hours, refueling in flight with the aid of a Douglas C-1 cargo-tanker.

The Fokker seats ten, plus a crew of two, and is powered by triple Armstrong Siddeleys developing a total of 645 hp. It has a top speed of 115 mph, a cruising speed of 93 mph, and a cruising range of 477 miles

De Havilland *Moth*

This immensely successful biplane is a low-cost sporting aircraft that has benefited from numerous improvements over its production run. Later versions, with improved engines, are dubbed the *Gypsy Moth* and *Tiger Moth*. A *Gypsy Moth* piloted by Amy Johnson accomplishes the first England to Australia solo flight made by a woman. Thousands of these aircraft are destined to see service as basic trainers in the early days of the Second World War.

Seating two, and usually powered by a 60 hp Cirrus engine, the Moth reaches a top speed of 90 mph, and has a cruising range of 150 miles.

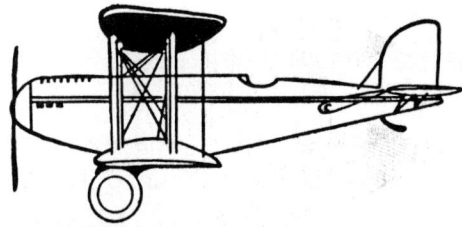

Ford 4-AT Trimotor

Although similar in appearance to the three-engine Fokker F.VII, the Ford monoplane incorporates a unique corrugated metal skin coated with non-corrosive aluminum providing exceptional durability. This innovation gives rise to the plane's nickname, the "Tin Goose." Other design innovations include wheel brakes and a tail wheel in place of the simple skid. Although the passenger compartment is noisy—like most trimotor designs—this aircraft provides the finest in state-of-the-art air passenger transportation. A Ford trimotor with modified wingspan and oversized fuel tanks, named the "Floyd Bennett," carries Richard Byrd and Bernt Balchin over the South Pole in November of 1929.

Seating a crew of two plus fourteen passengers, the 4-AT is powered by Wright engines producing a total of 900 hp. The plane has a top speed of 130 mph, and a cruising range of 1140 miles. Although production ceases in 1932 when the design is made obsolete by larger, twin-engine designs, the durable "Tin Goose" is a familiar sight in the skies for decades to come.

Aircraft Performance Figures

PERFORMANCE FIGURES for aircraft vary greatly depending on the types of engines used, loading, etc. The following figures were compiled by the British RAF using aircraft designed near the end of the decade. These figures can be used to roughly estimate the performance of similarly sized and powered aircraft.

Crew indicates the number of airmen required to properly operate the aircraft; *HP* is the total horsepower of the engine(s); *Weight* is the total weight of the aircraft loaded with crew and fuel; *Surface* is the total lifting surface of the wings expressed in square feet; *Cargo* is the total additional weight the aircraft can safely carry above the gross weight; *TS* indicates top speed, the maximum speed the aircraft can obtain and usually 20-25% above normal recommended cruising speed; *Climb* is the maximum rate of climb expressed in feet per minute to an altitude of 6500 feet (note that the rate of ascent decreases as altitude is gained and the atmosphere thins); *Ceiling* is the aircraft's 'service ceiling,' the altitude above which the aircraft's rate of climb drops below 100 feet per minute.

Aircraft Crew	Crew	HP	Weight	Surface	Cargo	TS	Climb	Ceiling
1-seat Fighter	1	394	2946	293	351	154	1635	27,100
1-seat Bomber	2	670	7773	695	1034	122	790	18,000
2-engine Bomber	3	964	8852	964	1057	130	970	23,500
Night Bomber	4	940	18,460	2164	3104	93	135	7600
General Purpose	2	482	4240	488	540	132	955	22,700
Recon Seaplane	3	470	5300	443	574	130	800	18,900
Flying Boat	5	940	14,300	1447	2059	101	323	14,300

Lockheed *Vega*

This single-engine, high winged monoplane was specifically designed for the civilian market and first appears in 1927. Flown and endorsed by such renowned pilots as Amelia Earhart and Wiley Post, a *Vega* is the first aircraft to make a successful eastward crossing of the Arctic, flying from Point Barrow, Alaska, to Spitsbergen, north of Norway. In 1933 Wiley Post uses a *Vega* to make a much-publicized solo flight around the world.

The Vega seats one crew member and six passengers, and is powered by a 450 hp Pratt & Whitney engine . It has cruising speed of 170 mph, and a range of 550 miles.

Aircraft Accessories

Potential pilots will want to purchase a padded aviator's helmet ($4.98), goggles ($2.49), and possibly a lined leather jacket ($8.95), all available from military surplus stores. A white silk scarf is optional, costing anywhere from $1.49 to $2.49.

Parachutes

Parachutes come into general use around 1921, although German pilots made use of them in the last days of the War. The seat pack, developed by the U.S. Army in 1919 has proven the most popular. Weighing 18 lbs., it is worn across the buttocks and serves as a seat cushion when flying. Back pack models and lap models are also available, sometimes preferred by airman whose duties require them to move around. Made almost entirely of silk, parachutes cost $35.95 to $45.95. They consist of a main chute 22-28 feet in diameter, and a small pilot chute, three feet in diameter, that emerges first and pulls the main chute free. Parachutes are properly packed when purchased. Repacking a chute must be done properly in order to insure that it fits back into its canvas pack, and can deploy properly when next used.

Military surplus also made available parachute flares. Normal, fast-burning flares attached to parachutes can be dropped from a plane and used to illuminate large areas, making possible the search for suspects or the taking of photographs. Parachute flares cost $1.95 each.

Armament

Airplanes are easily adapted for combat. Many were originally military designs, and others can be fitted as desired. Machine guns are favored weapons, the Browning, Vickers, and Lewis gun among the most popular. Military fighters had mechanical synchronizer that timed the machine gun's bullets to pass safely between the blades of the whirling propeller, allowing fighter pilots to sit directly behind their weapons. It is unlikely that any sort of synchronizer can be devised for a civilian craft. In this case, machine guns can be mounted on the wing above the cockpit, or, on open-cockpit planes, mounted on a swivel and fired to the rear by a second-seat passenger. Lightweight Lewis guns were often used in this capacity.

Aerial bombs are presently being manufactured and stockpiled in sizes weighing up to 4000 pounds. At two tons, and standing nearly sixteen feet high, it is unlikely that any plane available to an investigator could lift it. However, smaller bombs, some as light as 15-25 lbs., can be easily dropped by hand from an open cockpit or window. Although not generally available, they might be found on the weapons' black-market. ∎

Skill—Parachuting

ANYONE CAN BE TAUGHT the fundamentals of using a parachute in just a few minutes. Making sure that straps are cinched tight (especially between the legs), and knowing how to pull the ripcord is all that is necessary for the novice to make an emergency parachute leap. The two prescribed ways of safe jumping are 'lift-off' and 'free-fall.' Both require the parachuter to climb out on a wing until he is sure to clear the tail section of the aircraft. With the lift-off method, the jumper holds onto the plane while pulling the ripcord, allowing the drag of the emerging chute to pull him free. Free-fall parachuting involves jumping from the aircraft and falling a certain distance before pulling the ripcord and deploying the chute. Although there is concern about the effects of extended free-fall, 4000-foot falls have been made without any apparent ill effects.

Parachutes require a minimum of 150 feet to fully deploy and become effective; 250 feet is considered the safe minimum altitude. Parachute jumps as high as 25,000 feet have been successfully made.

Proper, and safe parachuting calls for a specific skill. Anyone can be shown the basics in a few minutes, and be awarded a starting skill of 20%. Only experience gained jumping improves the skill.

A falling parachute sometimes begins oscillating. If unchecked, the chute can rock too far and collapse. Oscillation can be controlled by pulling the shroud lines in a way that damps the inertia of the rocking chute.

Parachutes can be steered to a degree. By pulling the shroud lines down on a particular side, the chute tends to sideslip in that direction. Note that this method increases the rate of descent and should be avoided when nearing the ground. This method can allow a parachuter to avoid trees, tall buildings, or power lines.

Smooth landings insure an uninjured jumper. A parachuter falls at a rate of 16 to 24 feet per second, depending on his weight, the impact the equivalent of a jump from a height of 4 to 9 feet. The natural tendency is to underestimate the distance to the ground, resulting in the jumper pulling his legs up too soon and landing in a bad position. Sudden crosswinds at ground level can yank a chute sideways and turn an ankle if the touchdown is rough. Parachuting into water is most safely done by unstrapping oneself when low over the water, then jumping clear of the chute when six to ten feet above the water's surface. This also requires the Parachute skill.

Lastly, once on the ground, a strong wind can billow out a chute and possibly drag a jumper across the ground. A successful Parachute skill allows the jumper to quickly and efficiently collapse the chute.

PART-4

Equipment & Arms

Everyday Items, Heavier Equipment, Detective Gear,
Camping Equipment, Favorite american candies, Winter Gear,
Artificial Illumination, Observation, Photography, Movies,
Recording and Communication, Climbing Gear, Weapons.

SOME TYPE OF EQUIPMENT is necessary to almost any investigation, and defending oneself often a top priority. The following chapter discusses commonly available equipment, and provides a description of different weapons, including an intensive look at firearms.

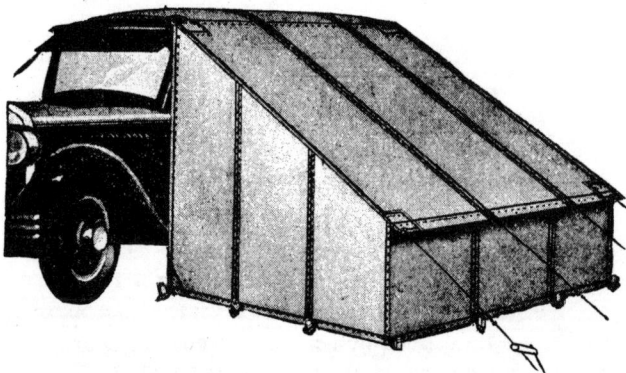

Sears Car Tent

Everyday Items

There are a number of everyday objects most investigators will, or should, carry. Aside from obvious functions, many can serve other purposes as well.

Although wristwatches are becoming more popular, a large pocket watch can also be used as a sundial, orienting a lost investigator. Watches, like any personal jewelry, can in a pinch be used as bribes. As for other valuables, investing in a secure money belt is not a bad idea. Small pocket mirrors, the kind kept in ladies' handbags, are useful when checking for signs of life in a corpse, flashing emergency signals out of doors, or spying around corners.

Keep a small note pad and pencil on hand. A multiple-blade jackknife is also recommended; models with dozens of different blades and tools are available. A short tape measure comes in handy, along with a piece of chalk for marking. A magnifying glass is always useful, and small, folding telescopes that fit in a breast pocket are handy out-of-doors. A waterproof box of matches is always a safe bet.

Heavier Equipment

Many investigators keep a standard list of heavy equipment stored in the trunk of their automobile, ready for emergencies. Normal inventories consist of shovels and picks, bolt-cutters, crowbars, toolbox with nippers and hacksaw, first aid kit, and rope. Travel guides, maps, and perhaps a local field guide are also recommended. A couple long-burning flares can be of use in emergencies.

Detective Gear

A pair of handcuffs may come in handy, and a professional set of locksmith's tools might also be of use. Prices for the latter range from $15 for an apprentice kit, to $45 for a set of precision tools in a leather case. Amateur fingerprint kits with brushes, two kinds of powder, and instruction book cost as little as $5.

Camping Equipment

Spurred by private auto ownership, camping is currently a popular vacation alternative. A wide selection of equipment is readily available.

Canvas tents range in price from $5.95 to nearly $50, ranging in size from 7' x 7' up to 16' x 24'. One model, selling for $14.95, attaches to the side of a parked automobile. Gas-powered camp stoves cost $4-$10, aluminum cook kits for four under $5. Vacuum bottles to keep drinks cold or hot cost $1.09. Sleeping bags are not yet popular, but there are wide variety of folding camp beds for $5-$10, mattresses costing an additional $4-$8. Folding cots run less than $3, and folding camp chairs and stools of canvas and wood less than a $1. A simple waterproof bedroll with camp blanket costs $4-$10. A folding bathtub can be had for $7.98. Sheath knives cost $1.79 to $2.48. A compass costs anywhere from 55 cents to $2.45 for the jeweled model. A pedometer, to keep track of distances hiked, costs $1.98.

Winter Gear

Snowshoes are $5.98 a pair. Skis cost $2.39 to $5.48 and bindings $1.98 a pair; poles go for 79 cents each. Ice skates cost $3.89 to $8.95 a pair.

Artificial Illumination

Whether camping or exploring caves, artificial light is essential. A variety of types are currently available.

Flares: Coming in disposable cardboard tubes, flares are ignited by twisting off their caps. Held aloft they throw a reasonably bright light and are of particular use when illuminating large chambers. Some come with spikes for mounting in the ground. Often used as emergency devices, they are available in a variety of colors aside from white. Price: 27 cents apiece.

Kerosene Lanterns: These lamps have been around for years. They throw a soft yellow light in all directions and burn from 4-8 hours on a single filling. Risky devices, they may explode if dropped or turned upside down. If submerged they must be disassembled, cleaned and dried, both wick and fuel replaced. Price: as cheap as $1.39.

Gas Lanterns: Manufactured by such companies as Coleman, Inc., these lanterns burn white gasoline, pressurized by a hand pump. They produce a brilliant, white light, larger units holding as much as a quart of gasoline and burning for 8-12 hours between refills—although they occasionally have to be pumped to maintain pressure. Although safer than kerosene lamps, gas lanterns are still quite fragile. Dropping one almost certainly means breaking either the mantles (wicks) and/or the surrounding globe. If dropped in water, the lantern is useless until disassembled, dried, and cleaned—a process taking at least a couple hours. Price: $5.48 with separate pump, $6.59 with built-in pump. Mantles cost 35 cents per half-dozen; extra mica globes 63 cents each.

Electric Torches: These lights are powered by electric dry cells and come in a variety of styles. Their light is weaker than gas-powered lanterns, and usually thrown in a beam. A fresh set of batteries keeps these devices burning for 2-4 hours, although the light tends to grow dimmer as the batteries expend themselves. If dropped, there is a 75% chance that the filament in the bulb breaks. If a spare is handy, replacement takes only a couple minutes. If dropped in water the flashlight must be taken apart, cleaned, dried, and reassembled, taking 5-10 minutes. Price: A single cell flashlight costs $1.35; a double cell model $2.25. These units weigh five and eight pounds, respectively. Extra batteries are 30 cents each, and bulbs 21 cents.

Carbide Lamps: These are the type used by miners and other professionals. They come in a wide variety of styles including lantern, bulls-eye lantern, flashlight, and mounted atop headgear. They generate a brilliant white light by burning acetylene gas produced by chemical car-

tridges. Carbide lights are the brightest of all and burn from 2-4 hours on a small cartridge, far longer on a large, belt-hung cartridge. If dropped, they are usually extinguished but easily relit, even if submerged in water. There is some danger from the open flame. Price: A small reflector lantern costs 89 cents, the better model with self-igniting apparatus, $1.55. A large lantern that throws a beam for 300 feet costs $2.59. The long-distance 'Hunters' model, with cap and belt-hung cartridge, costs $5.95. Two-pound carbide cans cost 27 cents, ten-pound containers $1.25.

Observation

In the field, long-distance lenses are useful. Small folding telescopes are good, but binoculars, with their wider field of range, are superior.

An achromatic telescope with x10 magnification and 30 yard width of field at 1000 yards costs $3.45. For x20 power, with 22 yard width of field, $5.95. At five and eight inches (closed) either slips easily into a coat pocket.

Opera glasses x2 power or less cost $3-$4. Field glasses with powers of x3 to x6 and width of fields from 40 to 75 yards (at 1000 yards) typically cost from $6-$13. An imported, high-quality pair of prism binoculars provide magnification of x8 and a superior width of field of 115 yards at 1000 yards. They cost $28.50.

x8 Prism Field Glasses

Photography

Cheap snapshot cameras are available from a number of manufacturers but the field is clearly dominated by the Eastman Kodak Company. Kodak Brownies are available in four models priced from $2.29 to $4.49, producing

Hawkeye Folding Cameras

prints sized between 2 1/4 x 3 1/4 inches and 2 7/8 x 4 7/8 inches. Better cameras, with folding bellows come in three different series ranging in price from $4.25 for a vest-pocket model to as much as $28.00 for the top of the line.

All snapshot film is black & white. Flashbulbs are not yet available and shooting indoors usually requires special lighting or flash powder, and Photography skill rolls. Light meters, tripods, lenses, and various filters are also available. Carrying cases of imitation leather cost anywhere from $1.80 to $2.25. Film costs 21 to 50 cents a roll, most with six exposures. Developing runs 9 cents a picture, 5 cents a print. Investigators wishing to do their own developing find a wide range of equipment available.

Movies

Amateur movie equipment has been around for some time but of standard 35mm size, it is cumbersome and high-priced. Kodak has recently introduced a new 16mm size. Cameras light enough to be held by hand are priced at $90, the projector for $70. Film costs $5.40 for a 100-foot roll including processing, which must be done by Kodak through the mail. Pathé of France has recently introduced a 9 1/2mm home movie film system.

Audio Recording

Recording tape has not yet been invented. Records are made by recording direct to a master disc. The only portable recording machines available are dictating machines like those made by Dictaphone, Inc.

The recording medium is a wax cylinder, rotated by a hand-cranked spring mechanism similar to a record player. The operator speaks into a horn, the signal recorded onto the cylinder. Playback is handled in a similar manner. Cylinders can be reused. A special device shaves them smooth, erasing past recordings and leaving a fresh surface for the next recording. A typical dictaphone costs $39.95.

Magnetic recording is in its infancy. Recording directly onto a spooled wire, the system is expensive. One interesting model, the Telegraphone (invented 1910), is attached to a telephone where it automatically records conversations. Wire recorders are powered by large batteries recharged off house current. A wire recorder costs $129.95, $149.95 for the Telegraphone.

Communication

Two-way radios are far too delicate and heavy for most field work, even if the problem of power supply could be overcome. Field telephones, connected by cables, and driven by either batteries or a hand-cranked generator, is the best system available. Cable is stored on a reel, ready to be quickly deployed as needed.

Radio receivers can be taken to the field. Most radios are powered by large rechargeable batteries, good for four to six hours.

Climbing Gear

Rope is available in hemp or cotton. Hemp is the superior performer—resistant to fraying, and nearly weatherproof, but exceedingly heavy and cumbersome to haul about. A 100-foot coil is about all that a person can comfortably carry. Cotton is much lighter, and more flexible, but more prone to failure, and possible disaster.

Mountaineering has been popular since the middle of the last century but available equipment is limited to crampons, (spikes fastened to boots), pitons (ice spikes), pickels (ice axes), and grappling hooks. Professionally made climbing shoes are unheard of. Most climbers make their own, driving nails through the soles of stout leather boots.

Professional linemen's equipment is available: climber's strap, $1.59; climbing spikes (attached to shoes), $1.98.

Miscellaneous

Bear trap, $11.43; padded leather football helmet, $3.65; canvas athletic shoes with crepe soles, $1.98; wheelchair, $27.30 to $33.30; 3-foot high floor safe (950 lbs.), $62.50; electric space heater, $1.98 to $2.98; desk phone, $14.95; telegraph key, $2.48 to $4.85; radio receiver, $54.95 to $115.00; battery eliminator for radio, $56.95; pocket microscope, $1.98; x250 desk microscope, $11.98; wet sponge respirator, $1.95; steno pads, 12 for 45 cents; tank-type sprayer, $4.85.

Self-Defense

DESPITE ALL PRECAUTIONS self-defense is sooner or later necessary. A brief overview of hand-to-hand weapons is followed by an extensive article on firearms.

Clubs

Clubs are generally divided into two categories, small and large, depending on whether they are wielded with one hand or two. Regardless, only a single Club skill is required. A club can be anything from a specifically designed police night stick, to a length of wooden 2 x 4, to a piece of pipe, to a baseball bat, to a shotgun or rifle. Clubs take advantage of character damage bonuses, and two-handed clubs can be used to Block (see *Skills*).

Clubs are particularly effective at knocking victims unconscious. If taken from behind, by surprise, a victim is stunned for 1D6 rounds if struck behind the head. A fumble might indicate an accidental serious injury, or even death.

Black Jack: 40%, 1D4+db.
Small Club, One-handed: 25%, 1D6+db.
Large Club, Two-Handed: 25%, 1D8+db.

The M-12 Billy

The M-12 Billy is a dual-function weapon. Aside from being used as a nightstick, the M-12 can also be loaded with a flare round (Handgun skill, 1D10+1D3 burn, Base Range 10 yards), 10-gauge shotgun round (see Firearms), or the M-12 tear gas cartridge.

M-12 'Billy': 25%, 1D6+db.

Military Fighting Knife

Knives

Knife fighting is a single skill applied to a wide variety of weapons. Knives come in many types, some designed specifically for combat; common types are listed below. All are capable of impaling, and because of the twisting, cutting methods of knife fighting, character damage bonuses also apply. Knives are too small for effective parrying.

Note that only specifically designed knives can be thrown effectively, and doing so requires a separate Throw Knife skill with a base chance of 10%.

Pocketknife: 25%, 1D3+db plus impale.
Switchblade: 25%, 1D4+db plus impale.
Hunting Knife: 25%, 1D6+db plus impale.
Commando Knife: 25%, 1D4+2+db plus impale.
Bowie Knife: 25%, 1D6+2+db plus impale.

Throwing Knife: 15%, 1D4+1+db plus impale; base range is STR x1 yards, maximum range STR x3 yards. A throwing knife can also be used as a hand-held knife.

Trench Knife: 25%, 1D6+1+db plus impale. From the Great War, this formidable fighting knife features a hilt with brass knuckles that inflicts an additional 2 points of damage with every successful Fist/Punch attack.

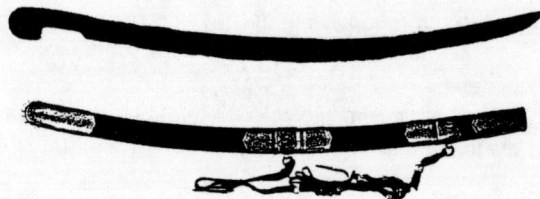

Cavalry Sabre

Swords

Although modern firearms have made swordsmanship almost obsolete, many investigators may still have trained with these weapons, either for sport or in the military. Note that sword fighting requires two separate skills, one for Attack, and a separate one for Parry. Both begin at the same percentage, but increase independently of each other.

Swords fall into two broad categories: light, thrusting weapons like foils and rapiers; and heavy, cutting, slashing weapons like sabres, cutlasses, broadswords, and scimitars. Piercing weapons can impale, but do not take advantage of character damage bonuses. Difficult to use effectively, base chance to hit or parry is 15%. Conversely, most slashing swords do not impale, but do take advantage of a character's damage bonus. Simpler in concept, these swords have base chances of 25% to either hit or parry.

Piercing Swords

Fencing Foil: 15%, 1D6+1 plus impale. This assumes the tip is unguarded and sharpened. Note that foils are incapable of piercing any opponent with armor of two points or more, the thin blade merely bending instead. Foils are designed for sport and do not make particularly effective weapons.

Sword Cane: 15%, 1D6 plus impale. A thrusting sword designed to fit inside an otherwise innocent looking walking stick. Intended for personal protection on the streets, it's balance is inherently bad, reducing its potential damage.

Rapier/Heavy Epee: 15%, 1D6+1 plus impale. A heavy piercing sword with a blade triangular in cross-section. These swords are designed as weapons and dangerous in skilled hands.

Cutting Swords

Machete: 25%, 1D8+db. A heavy-bladed weapon used in South America to hack paths through jungle. Technically a knife, the machete is used much the same way as a heavy sword.

Cavalry Sabre: 25%, 1D8+1+db. A very heavy one-handed sword with a single-edged, slightly curved blade. Although no longer used by most militaries they are a standard accessory with many dress uniforms.

Archery

Of tall, single-curve design, modern bows are little changed from the ancestral English long bow (composite bows and recurves do not appear until the mid to late 1930s). Although awkward and impossible to conceal, they do have the advantage of silence. Damage given assumes a broadhead hunting arrow; blunter target arrows do only 1D3 points. Either is capable of impaling.

The base range shown is for a bow with a 50-lb. pull, a typical hunting weight, and the kind an investigator might discover in an abandoned cabin. Note that the 'weight' of the bow affects both the base range and damage. Base range is figured at one yard per two pounds of pull. Note that, like firearms, point-blank range rules apply.

It requires strength to pull a bow. Multiply a character's STR x5 to determine the maximum (and proper) weight that character can pull. The weight of the bow can also affect the amount of damage, assuming the character is strong enough to pull it to its limit. Bows of 65 lbs. or greater do +1D4 points of damage; above 85 lbs., +1D6 points. Lightweight, juvenile bows of less than 35 lbs. do half the rolled damage. Note that no matter how strong a character might be, he can do no more damage than that particularly weight bow allows.

50 lb. Long Bow: 20%, 1D6 plus impale; base range 25 yards. An archer equipped with a quiver of arrows can fire once per round. The maximum effective range is the weight of the bow x4 yards; damage beyond that distance is halved.

Crossbows

Uncommon in the 1920s, a few are built by custom craftsmen in the U.S. and Europe. Others will simply be relics or antiques pulled down from their customary spot over the fireplace. Nearly silent, they are slow to fire. Reloading a light crossbow requires the user to place his foot in a stirrup and cock the weapon by pulling the string back with both hands; normal rate of fire is 1/2. A heavy crossbow is usually cocked by means of a hand-cranked winch; rate of fire is 1/4.

Light Crossbow: Rifle skill, 1D6+2; base range 60 yards.
Heavy Crossbow: Rifle skill, 1D8+2; base range 90 yards.

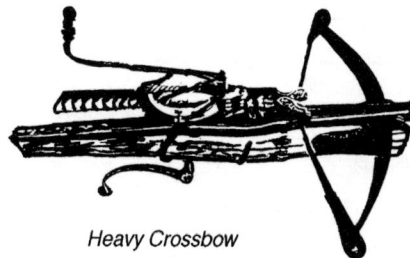

Heavy Crossbow

Maritime Weapons

Seagoing tools and equipment often serve double duty as weapons. Listed below are a few of the types found aboard ship.

Batten: Club skill, 1D6+db. A short, turned piece of wood, used to secure lines and hatches.

Boat Hook: Club or Spear skill, 1D8+db. A pole six to twelve feet long, with a pointed tip and hook.

Gaff: 25% (Hook skill), 1D4 plus impale. A short iron hook on a wooden handle.

Marlinespike: Knife skill, 1D3+db plus impale. A short iron spike with handle, used for splicing lines.

Paddle/Oar: Club skill, 1D6+db.

Seagoing Firearms

Flare Gun: Handgun skill, 1D10+2, plus may ignite flammable materials; base range 10 yards. A single-shot weapon, the most common model is the 1915 Remington. In addition to the normal flare round (misfire 96-00), it can also be loaded with a 10-gauge shotgun shell (see *Firearms*).

Line-Throwing Gun: Rifle skill, 1D8 plus impale; base range 30 yards, double the range if no line is attached.

Lyle Gun: 20% (Light Artillery skill), 3D6 plus impale; base range 100 yards, double if no line attached.

Sven Foyn Harpoon Gun: 20% (Light Artillery skill), 3D8 plus impale; base range 40 yards, doubled if no line attached. A heavy, deck-mounted weapon, this small can-

Weapons of Convenience

SUNDRY OBJECTS THAT, although not intended as weapons, serve the purpose when nothing else is at hand.

AXES

These weapons benefit from damage bonuses. Either can be thrown; Throw Axe/Hatchet is a separate skill with a base chance of 15%. Base range for either is STR x1 yard, maximum range STR x3 yards.

Wood Axe: Club skill, 1D8+2+db.
Hatchet or Hand Axe: Club skill, 1D6+1+db.

FROM THE TOOLBOX
Chisel: Knife skill, 1D2+db plus impale.
Crowbar: Club skill, 1D4+1.
Cutting Torch: Knife skill, 40%, 1D6 burn.
File/Rasp: Knife skill, 1D3+db plus impale.
Hammer: Club skill, 1D4+1+db.
Hoe: Club skill, 1D2+db.
Pickaxe: Club skill, 1D6+1+db plus impale.
Pipe Wrench: Club skill, 1D6+db.
Pitchfork: 20% / Bayonet/Spear skill, 1D8+db plus impale.
Rake: Club skill, 1D2+db.
Screwdriver: Knife skill, 1D2+db plus impale.
Scythe: Club skill, 1D8+1+db.
Shovel: Club skill, 1D3+db.
Sickle: Club skill, 1D6+1+db.
Sledge Hammer, Two-Handed: Club skill, 1D8+2+db.
Trowel: Knife skill, 1D3+db plus impale.

AROUND THE HOUSE
Bookcase, Toppled: variable, 1D6.
Cast Iron Skillet: Club skill, 1D3+db.
Chair/Bar Stool: Club skill, 1D6+db.
Cooking Fork: Knife skill, 1D3+db plus impale.
Fireplace Poker: Club skill, 1D6+db.
Flatiron: Club skill, 1D3+1+db.
Glass Bottle, Unbroken: Club skill, 1D3.
Glass Bottle, Broken: Knife skill, 1D4 plus impale.
Ice Pick: Knife skill, 1D2+db plus impale.
Knife, Butcher: Knife skill, 1D6+db plus impale.
Knife, Paring: Knife skill, 1D3+db plus impale.
Letter Opener: Knife skill, 1D2+db plus impale.
Live Wire, 110 Volts: touch, 1D8 plus stun.
Live Wire, 220 Volts: touch, 2D8 plus stun.
Meat Cleaver: Club skill, 1D4+1+db.
Meat Hook: 25% (Hook skill), 1D3 plus impale.
Meat Tenderizer: Club skill, 1D3+db.
Mirror: Club skill, 1D3+1D6 from cuts.
Scissors: Knife skill, 1D3+db plus impale.
Stairs, Knock Down: variable, 1D6+1D4 per flight.
Straight Razor: Knife skill, 1D3 plus impale.

MISCELLANEOUS
Brick: Club or Fist/Punch skill, 1D4+1+db.
Burning Torch/Flare: Club skill, 1D4+db+1D3 burn.
Chain: 20%, 1D4+1+db.
Rock, Thrown: Throw skill, 1D4, base range is STR x1 yard, maximum range STR x5 yards.

non is used in the whaling industry. A 220 grain charge fires a harpoon weighing over 100 pounds, carrying a heavy line.

In addition to damage done by the harpoon, an explosive charge goes off three seconds after impact, causing 3D10 damage, followed by four hinged, 12-inch barbs that spring out for another 4D6 points of damage.

Specialty Weapons

Bull Whip: 5%, 1D3 or entangle, 10-foot range. A character attempting to use a whip to entangle must indicate what he wishes to hit: legs, arm, weapon, head and throat, etc. If successful, apply STR vs. STR struggle and Grapple rules. A miss indicates no damage.

Garrotte: 15%, strangle. A deadly weapon of assassination, the garotte must be used from behind on an unsuspecting victim. If the attack is successful, apply Drowning rules.

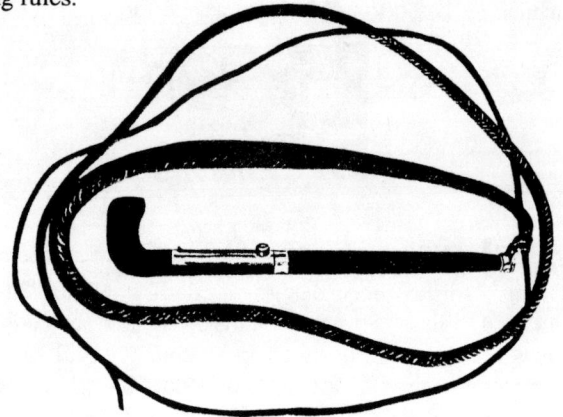

Unusual Weapons

Although the following weapons are by no means common, investigators may possess them as heirlooms or antiques, or come across them in the course of their adventures.

Spears and Lances

Spears (or javelins) are usually lighter weapons, intended to be thrown or used in hand-to-hand combat. Lances are heavier, often intended to be used from horseback. Although lances make a formidable weapon on foot they are generally too heavy to throw. All spears and lances can impale. In hand-to-hand combat they take advantage of damage bonuses and can be used to Parry as well (a separate skill with a base chance of 20%).

Damages shown are for the 'average' weapon and could be increased to as much as 1D10+1 for a broadheaded African ashanti, or reduced to 1D4 for a sharpened and fire-hardened stick. Damage bonuses only apply if the spear is used in hand to hand combat, not when thrown. Note that when used from charging horseback, or planted firmly against a charging opponent, a spear or lance does an additional 1D6 points of damage (although damage bonuses do not apply). Successfully using a lance from horseback may require a Ride skill as well as Lance.

Spear or Lance: 20% (Bayonet/Spear skill), 1D8+1+db.

Thrown Spear: 20% (Throw Spear/Javelin skill), 1D8+1+db; base range is STR x2 yards, maximum range is STR x4 yards. Note that many primitives use spear-throwers made of wood, bone, or antler. These devices double the range of the weapon, but using one requires a separate skill distinct from normal Throw Spear; base chance with a spear-thrower is 10%.

Miscellaneous

Hunting or War Boomerang: 10% (Boomerang skill), 1D8; base range is STR x5 yards, maximum range is STR x10 yards. Figures assume the weapon is a hunting or war boomerang perhaps three feet long. Larger versions up to six feet long, used by aboriginal Australians, do as much as 1D10+2 points. Although their flight is curved, these boomerangs are not designed to return to the thrower.

Blowgun: 25%, 1 point of damage plus impale; base range 15 yards. A primitive weapon consisting of a hollow tube from which a small dart is fired by a puff of air. The dart is usually tipped with poison or a sedative drug. Typical blowguns are nearly ten feet in length although shorter versions are sometimes encountered, with commensurately reduced base ranges.

Bolos: 10%, 1D4 plus entangle; base range is STR x2 yards, maximum range STR x6 yards. Usually three heavy balls attached together with leather cords. Whirled above the head and thrown, a successful cast entangles the legs of a running target, bringing it to the ground. Bolos are used by the gauchos of the Argentine Pampas as well as others. A fumbled throw results in a painful injury.

Quoit: 25%, 1D6+1; base range is STR x3 yards, maximum range is STR x5 yards. Flat metal rings used as weapons in India. The edges are sharpened in order to inflict maximum damage.

Throwing Stars: 20%, 1D2 plus impale; base range is STR x2 yards, maximum range is STR x4 yards. Of Asian origin, throwing stars are of flat metal, armed with a variety of points, barbs, and cutting edges. It is possible to tip them with poisons or drugs.

Nunchuks: 5%, 1D4 (x2). Also of Asian origin nunchuks are basically a pair of clubs connected by a short chain. Difficult to use, a fumble always results in some minor injury.

Firearms

ALTHOUGH RARELY IN and of themselves the best solution to a problem, personal firearms are a favored form of self-defense. A vast array of weapons are available; some of the more common are discussed below.

A Note About These Rules

This section expands considerably on firearms descriptions and rules found in various editions of *Call of Cthulhu*. Variations from the original rules are few, and mostly minor, requiring little adjustment by players and providing no threat to game balance. Although these rules are necessary to accurately describe the various types of firearms in use today, they generally are not required for play. Keepers and players may elect to retain the simpler, original rules, retaining only the descriptions to provide atmosphere and realism. Most rule changes amount to additions that highlight subtle differences. These additions can be adopted as wished, using some, ignoring others.

.44 Revolver

Firearms Tables

Some of the more common firearms are described in detail; additional weapons are listed on the tables. Note that the lists and descriptions omit a number of the essential statistics including Damage, Attacks per Round, and Base Range. For numerous reasons these statistics must be derived from the *Firearms Tables* found at the end of the chapter. Although this method takes a little more time it allows for a more detailed description. Alternatively, players may elect to use a simpler approach, simply ex-

Savage Model 1917
.32 cal. Automatic

Handguns

PISTOLS ARE A favored weapon. Easily concealed, deadly at close range, and quickly disposed of when necessary, they are inexpensive and easy to obtain.

Although derringers and a few others are single-shot weapons, most handguns are revolvers or semiautomatics—the latter commonly called 'automatics.' Although more delicate, and hence more prone to jams, semiautomatics usually make use of magazines that load directly into the grip, allowing for faster reloading than revolvers. Most revolvers must be opened up and spent cartridges manually ejected before fresh rounds are loaded one-by-one into the separate chambers. Also, semiautomatics are almost always equipped with one or more safeties, while revolvers, with one or two exceptions, almost invariably lack them.

Most short barreled semiautomatics can be carried in a shoulder holster hidden under a jacket or coat, but long-barrel guns or large frame weapons like .45's leave noticeable bulges. Shoving the gun into one's belt, front or back, is a reasonable alternative. Ankle holsters can be used for small pistols but are not always convenient.

Special Ammunition

Hollow point bullets—also called dum-dums—are designed for hunting, and especially suitable for pistols. The slug breaks up upon entering the target, causing +2 damage. Armored targets, however, take only half the rolled damage, the hollow-point disintegrating on impact. This ammunition is banned by the Geneva convention but still favored by hunters and law enforcement agencies.

Wadcutter ammo looks like a normal bullet with the tip cut off. The blunt end inflicts a bonus damage of +2 points. However, the design is ballistically unstable and base range is typically reduced by half.

Options

Some military handguns are designed to accept a detachable shoulder stock, converting the pistol to a 'semi-carbine.' Base range is doubled but the shooter must use his Rifle skill.

Silencers, although available both commercially and home-made, are still rather primitive. They are ineffective on higher-powered firearms (with muzzle velocities exceeding 1100 feet per second) and do not work at all on revolvers, where noise escapes from around the rotating chamber anyway. The most likely candidate for a silencer is a semiautomatic pistol no larger than .45 caliber. Not as quiet as some might think, the sound of a 'silenced' .45 fired in another room has been described as sounding like

trapolating their weapon's statistics from similar examples found in the *Call of Cthulhu* rules.

This method also allows players to derive reasonably accurate statistics for firearms not included on the lists: weapons found in old magazine ads or in reference books. A few essentials such as caliber and barrel length—translated through the Firearms Tables—should provide a fair representation of the weapon.

It is always the final decision of the keeper whether to use the expanded rules, the simpler original rules, or any combination of the two.

Firearms and the Law

HANDGUNS, RIFLES, and shotguns are sold over the counter in most parts of the U.S. without license or registration. Restrictions are few and such things as fully automatic weapons and sawed-off shotguns are often perfectly legal.

During the 1920s the Federal Government did little to regulate firearms other than in 1927 to prohibit the shipping of handguns through the U.S. mail. Local communities, however, passed their own laws. Discharging a firearm within village or city limits without just cause is usually prohibited. Other restrictions vary widely. In the long-established Eastern states, particularly along the coast, restrictions are greatest. Carrying a concealed firearm is generally a felony. Laws are generally more lax in rural areas where firearms conceivably serve a more useful purpose, parts of the rural Midwest and South generally more lenient than the East. In parts of the West, private citizens and corporations accumulate arsenals containing machine guns and other heavy weapons. In Texas, Oklahoma, Arizona, New Mexico, and other parts, carrying a holstered sidearm in public is not at all uncommon.

Concealed firearms are generally closely regulated. Most communities are willing to license certain individuals to carry concealed weapons: usually professionals (detective, bodyguard, etc.), or because the person routinely moves valuables (banker, jeweler, shopkeeper). If the applicant passes the check (usually requiring a clean record—no felonies), a small fee is paid and the permit issued. He is required to carry the permit whenever carrying the weapon. The ease of obtaining a concealed weapons permit depends on community standards.

"someone slamming a dictionary down on a desktop." Silencers reduce base range by half and cause barrels to foul quickly with unejected, burnt powder. They also wear out rather quickly, growing louder with each firing, most rendered useless after 25+1D10 shots.

Some Suggested Handguns

Double Derringer

Remington Double Derringer M95

A classic double-barrel derringer design, over 150,000 were produced between 1866 and 1935. The M95 possesses a pair of round, over-and-under barrels, each firing a .41 rimfire short round. Although the two barrels cannot be fired simultaneously, they are easily both discharged in the space of a single round. Rather inaccurate, base range is 3 yards.

The first derringer was designed around 1850 by Philadelphia gunsmith Henry Deringer, Jr. The design was copied by many manufacturers who were careful to respell the name to avoid trademark difficulties.

Colt Single Action Army Revolver M1873

Called "the Peacemaker" or the "Frontier Six-Shooter," the single-action Colt is an Old West classic. The classic caliber is a .45 but the weapon was also made in a wide variety ranging from .22 rimfire on up. The most common barrel lengths are the 4.75-inch Civilian and the 7.5-inch Cavalry models, but the famous "Buntline Special" featured a custom-made 12-inch barrel. In production until 1940, this sidearm is used extensively in the military, law enforcement, and civilian sectors.

Colt Double Action Revolver M1877

Manufactured between 1877 and 1909 over 165,000 copies of this model were produced in two versions: the .38 Lightning and .41 Thunderer. Most feature checkered rosewood grips and a blued finish, though some are nickel plated. Barrel lengths range from 1.5 inches to 10 inches. Despite its popularity, its double-action system is overly complex and subject to malfunctions, sometimes deteriorating to the point where the weapon will only function as a single-action revolver.

Colt .45 Automatic M1911

First adopted by the military in 1911 this popular handgun is available in two versions: the M1911, and the M1911A1, virtually identical except for the A1's grip safety, making it safer to carry. Millions of this pistol have been manufactured around the world, serving in numerous wars as well as the law enforcement and civilian sectors. Using the powerful .45 ACP round, this gun has excellent stopping power. It has a seven-round detachable box magazine that loads into the grip. It is extremely reliable even under adverse conditions.

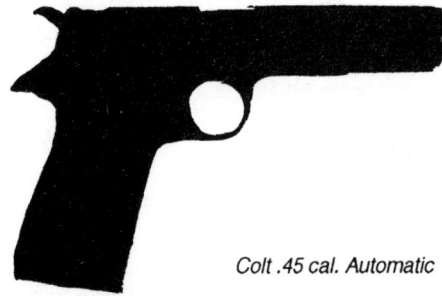

Colt .45 cal. Automatic

Mauser 'Broomhandle' Pistol M1912

One of the most distinctive handguns ever produced, the semiautomatic 'Broomhandle' takes its name from its narrow wooden grip. The Mauser first appeared in 1896 and has been constantly updated since. Manufactured in several different countries, it is available in a range of calibers including 9mm Parabellum and a Chinese version that accepts .45 ACP's. A Spanish version, the Astra M900, appears in 1928. Most models accept a shoulder stock.

The slender grip is too small to house a magazine which is instead mounted in front of the trigger guard. Clumsy to handle and expensive to manufacture, by the time of the World War the Broomhandle was relegated to secondary troops. In the 1920s they are used mostly by law enforcement personnel and security troops.

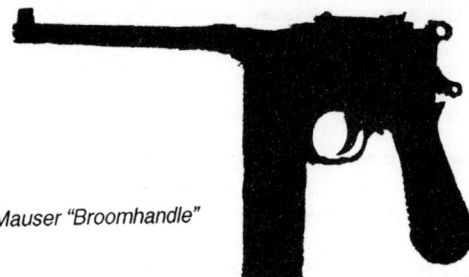

Mauser "Broomhandle"

PO8 Luger Pistol

This famous 9mm semiautomatic was used by Germany in the World War. A replacement for the Broomhandle Mauser, it remains in service throughout this decade and into the next. Comfortable to hold and use, the Luger's one drawback is its susceptibility to the dirt and grime of the battlefield.

A Selection of Handguns

Make/Model	Country	Year	Caliber	Action	Loading	Capacity	HP	Price
Astra M1921	Spain	1921	9mm Largo	semi	mag	8	8	$30
Beretta M1915	Italy	1915	.32 ACP/9mm Glisenti	semi	mag	7	8	$25/$30
Beretta M1919 (M418)	Italy	1919	.25 ACP	semi	mag	8	6	$20
Browning (FN) M1910	Belgium	1910	.32 ACP/.380 ACP	semi	mag	7	8	$25/$30
Campo-Giro M1913-16	Spain	1913	9mm Largo	semi	mag	8	8	$30
Colt Single Action Army Revolver	USA	1872	many	rev-1	side	6	10	$30
Colt M1877 'Lightning'	USA	1877	.38 Colt	rev	side	6	10	$25
Colt M1877 'Thunderer'	USA	1877	.41 Colt	rev	side	6	10	$28
Colt New Army and Navy Revolver	USA	1892	.38 Colt/.41 Colt	rev	swng	6	10	$25/$28
Colt New Service D.A. Revolver	USA	1898	.38 Colt	rev	swng	6	10	$25
Colt Positive Police Revolver	USA	1905	.32 Colt Long/.38 S&W	rev	swng	6	10	$15/$25
Colt M1908 Hammerless	USA	1908	.25 ACP/.380 ACP	semi	mag	6/7	6	$20/$30
Colt M1911 Pistol	USA	1911	.45 ACP	semi	mag	7	8	$40
Colt M1917 U.S. Army Revolver	USA	1917	.45 Colt/.45 ACP	rev	swng w/clip	6	10	$30
CZ Model 24	Czech	1924	.380 ACP	semi	mag	8	8	$30
CZ Model 27	Czech	1927	.32 ACP	semi	mag	8	8	$25
Enfield .38 No. 2 Mark I	UK	1927	.38 Webley	rev	brek	6	10	$30
Japanese Type 26 Revolver	Japan	1893	9mm Type 26	rev	brek	6	10	$25
Japanese M1904 Nambu	Japan	1904	8mm M1904	semi	mag	8	8	$25
Luger PO8 Pistol	Germany	1908	9mm Parabellum	semi	mag	8	8	$30
Mannlicher M1905	Argentina	1905	7.65mm Mann.	semi	clip	8	8	$25
Mauser 'Broomhandle' M1912	Germany	1896	7.63mm Mauser/9mm	semi	clip	10	8	$25/$30
Mauser M1910	Germany	1910	.25 ACP/.32 ACP	semi	mag	9/8	8	$20/$25
Nagant M1895 Revolver	Russia	1895	7.62mm M95	rev	side	7	10	$25
Remington Double Derringer (M95)	USA	1866	.41 rimfire	2-shot	brek	2	5	$15
Savage M1907 Pocket Auto Pistol	USA	1907	.32 ACP	semi	mag	8	8	$25
Savage M1917 Pistol	USA	1920	.32 ACP/.380 ACP	semi	mag	10/9	8	$15/$25
Smith & Wesson .38 D.A. 2nd Model	USA	1880	.38 S&W	rev	brek	5	10	$25
Smith & Wesson M1917 Army Rev.	USA	1917	.45 Colt/.45 ACP	rev	swng w/clip	6	10	$30
Smith & Wesson M1926 Military Rev.	USA	1926	.44 Special	rev	swng	6	10	$30
Star M1919 Pocket Pistol	Spain	1919	.25 ACP	semi	mag	8	6	$20
Star Model A	Spain	1924	9mm Largo	semi	mag	8	8	$30
Walther Model 1	Germany	1908	.25 ACP	semi	mag	6	6	$20
Walther Model PP	Germany	1929	.32 ACP	semi	mag	8	8	$25
Webley Mark I	UK	1887	.455 Webley	rev	brek	6	10	$30
Webley Mark II Police Model	UK	1897	.38 S&W	rev	brek	6	10	$25
Webley-Fosbery Automatic Revolver	UK	1901	.38 Colt Auto/.455 Webley	semi	brek	8/6	10	$50
Webley Automatic M1913	UK	1912	.455 Webley Auto	semi	mag	7	10	$40

Firearms Terminology and Abbreviations

FIREARMS ARE LISTED alphabetically by *Make* and *Model*, followed by the *Country* of manufacture, and the *Year* the firearm was first produced. *Caliber, Action, Loading, Capacity,* and *Hit Points* are all described below. *Price* is the approximate cost of a new firearm of that type.

BASE RANGE
A comparative measure of the accuracy ranges of different types of firearms. Note that this number does not indicate the maximum useful range of a weapon, only the distance beyond which the shooter's firearm skill is reduced. High-powered military rifles have effective ranges of up to 600 yards, and have even killed at distances greater than a mile.

CALIBER
Refers to the size (and type) of ammunition the gun is chambered for (for shotguns, see **Gauge**). The number is the diameter of the slug expressed in inches or millimeters. A second number, usually separated by a hyphen, identifies the specific design, sometimes indicating the powder load or even the year the cartridge was introduced. It is important to note that most firearms accept and fire only a single type of cartridge. For example, there are various 9mm cartridges but each is different and your firearm will accept only that particular cartridge for which it was designed. Some of the weapons on the firearms lists show more than one caliber. This only means that this particular firearm was manufactured in a number of different calibers, not that this weapon accepts all these calibers. Attempting to use an incorrect cartridge results in jams, failures, or even explosions.

An exception to the above rule are .22's. Many .22 caliber rifles and handguns are capable of firing all three common cartridges: shorts, longs, and long rifles.

GAUGE
The measure of shotguns (in England: *bore*). Shotguns were originally measured by the number of lead balls (the diameter of the barrel) required to equal a pound in weight. Hence, the smaller the gauge number, the larger and more powerful the weapon.

ACTION
The type of cocking mechanism: lever-action, revolver, semiautomatic, etc. Note that some actions are faster than others though slower, simpler designs are often more reliable.

Automatic (auto): Means 'fully automatic.' By simply depressing the trigger and holding it down, the firearm continuously fires until the trigger is released, or the magazine emptied. Note that many rifles and shotguns, and particularly handguns, are called "automatics" when in fact they are actually semiautomatics (see below). With a few exceptions, most fully automatic weapons of this era are either machine guns or submachine guns.

Bolt-action (bolt): Usually found on rifles and some shotguns. Simple and reliable, it requires a minimum amount of movement from the shooter.

Double-barrel (doub): A double-barrel weapon, usually a shotgun. They function similar to single-shot weapons.

Lever-action (levr): Most often found on rifles, and again, a few shotguns. One of the earliest types, the mechanism requires a good deal of movement to cock.

Pump-action (pump): Sometimes called slide-action, this was the first improvement over earlier, lever-action designs and commonly found on rifles and shotguns. Fresh rounds are chambered by sliding a grip that runs along the underside of the barrel.

Revolving-action (rev): A common handgun design, a revolving cylinder holds as many as six cartridges or more, rotating to bring fresh cartridges into firing position. Revolvers are of two designs: modern, double action (**rev**), and the older, single-action (**rev(s)**). The single action revolver is a slower, simpler design. Firing the weapon rotates the cylinder to a fresh round, but the weapon must then be manually cocked, usually by pulling the lever back with the thumb. With a double-action revolver the weapon also cocks itself, allowing the shooter to fire as fast as he can pull the trigger. Trigger pull of a double-action revolver is, predictably, a little harder.

Select (sel): This indicates the firearm has a selector switch that allows the weapon to be operated in either semiautomatic or fully automatic mode.

Semiautomatic (semi): Refers to a weapon that uses either mechanical action or gas pressure to eject spent cartridges, chamber fresh ones, and cock itself. A shot is fired with every squeeze of the trigger, and with less pull than required for double-action revolvers. Almost all "automatic" pistols are actually semiautomatics.

Single-shot (sing): The simplest type of design, a single round is loaded into the weapon, then fired. The spent cartridge must be removed and a fresh round inserted before firing again. Note that most double-barrel shotguns are essentially two single-shot weapons mounted on a single stock.

LOADING
Different guns are loaded in different ways. Some methods are faster, others offer simplicity and reliability.

Belt (belt): Used exclusively in automatic weapons, belts made of tough fabric or metal links are pre-loaded with cartridges then fed into machine guns to provide long periods of sustained fire. Old belts deteriorate, often resulting in jams.

Break-open (brek): Applies most often to revolvers and shotguns. Unlatched, the gun 'breaks in half' on a hinge, the barrel(s) tilting down exposing the chamber(s). Empty shells are removed and fresh cartridges loaded by hand. On some weapons spent casings are ejected automatically upon opening.

Clip (clip): Also called 'stripper clips' or 'chargers.' These small metal clips are preloaded with cartridges and carried separate from the weapon. Note that these differ from 'magazines' which are often erroneously called 'clips' (see below). Clips are most often used in semiautomatic pistols and some rifles, providing a fast means of reloading a spent weapon. Although an integral part of a weapon's design, a clip is not necessary to fire the weapon. Single cartridges can be loaded directly into the chamber and the weapon fired single-shot style.

Drum (drum): Essentially a large magazine (see below) holding an increased number of cartridges.

Magazine (mag): In this instance, the definition of magazine is a small metal box (often incorrectly called a 'clip') that is preloaded with ammunition then inserted into the weapon. Unlike clip weapons, magazine weapons usually incorporate an automatic safety that keeps the gun from firing when no magazine is in place. The result is that even with a round loaded directly into the chamber, the weapon will not fire unless a magazine has been installed. Like clips, extra magazines can be loaded ahead of time and carried separate from the weapon, allowing for fast reloading. Pistol magazines usually slide inside the handgrip.

Many rifles, shotguns, and other weapons also have 'magazines,' but of a non-detachable type. These are designated on the tables as "side-loading." Only those weapons denoted as magazine-type (mag) benefit from the quick reloading advantage of a detachable magazine.

Side-loading (side): This is a slower method, requiring that cartridges be fed one at a time into a small opening. Although most rifles and shotguns using this method automatically eject spent casings, side-loading revolvers require that spent casings be removed by hand.

Strip (strp): For machine guns. This method is sometimes used in place of belts. Smaller, and holding less rounds, strips are easier to feed into a machine gun and less prone to jams.

Swing-out (swng): Found only on revolvers, this design allows the entire cylinder to swing out on a hinge. Spent casings can be quickly dumped out and empty chambers reloaded one at a time.

CAPACITY
The maximum number of cartridges a firearm normally holds. Note that revolvers—for safety's sake—should be carried with an empty chamber under the firing pin, reducing the risk of accident, and reducing the capacity of the weapon by one. Although not a safe practice, most other actions (save single-shot type weapons) allow for the insertion of an extra round into the chamber, increasing the listed capacity by one.

HIT POINTS
This is indicative of the ruggedness of the weapon. Hit points are usually only inflicted on a weapon when it is used as a club, or to block some powerful blow. If hit points are exceeded, the gun may be destroyed or simply rendered unusable until repairs are made, depending on the situation.

Many variants are produced with barrel lengths from 4 to 12 inches. Longer-barrel versions mount a 32-round 'snail' drum in place of the standard eight-round magazine. Many Lugers accept shoulder stocks as well.

Webley-Fosbery Automatic Revolver

A unique weapon, the Webley uses the force of its recoil to rotate the chamber rather than trigger-pull, making it the only semiautomatic revolver on the market. Despite rejection by the British military, it is manufactured up until 1939 in both .38 and .455 calibers. The Webley-Fosbery is prone to jams unless kept clean but, unlike most revolvers, it features a safety.

Astra M1921

Based on the Camp-Giro M1913-16 pistol, the M1921 is unique in that it can chamber and fire a number of different rounds including the 9mm Browning Long, 9mm Glisenti, 9mm Largo, and 9mm Parabellum, as well as the .38 Super Auto cartridge (the Glisentis and Parabellums occasionally jam on well-worn weapons). The Astra is the standard sidearm of the Spanish army from 1921 on.

A Model M version appears in the 1930s chambered for the .45 ACP and with a selector switch allowing the pistol to be fired as a full automatic. Severe recoil makes it almost impossible to control.

Rifles

RIFLES ARE GENERALLY more powerful weapons with increased stopping power and superior range. Calibers range from .22 to .45 and larger, shoulder stocks providing steadier aim. Many rifles are produced in 'carbine' versions (originally intended for cavalry applications) that feature shorter barrels and smaller stocks. Base range is typically reduced to three-quarters normal, and magazine capacity is also often reduced.

Aside from simple single-shot models, rifles come in a wide variety of cocking and loading configurations. Lever-actions were first introduced in the mid-19th century. Pump-action (or slide-action) is a later variation that allows for steadier aim while cocking. Bolt-action is the choice of the military in this century. Rugged, it requires a minimum expenditure of move-

ment to operate. Semiautomatic rifles appeared earlier this century, allowing for faster rates of fire, but with mechanisms more vulnerable to dirt and jamming.

Most rifles are designed for military applications, only later being marketed to hunters and other sportsmen. The exception is rifles of .22 caliber, which fall into two rough categories: inexpensive 'youth rifles' of economical construction; and ultra-expensive target rifles, usually single-shot, and costing more than many high-powered rifles.

Special Ammunition

Hollow point and wadcutter ammunition similar to that used in handguns is available for smaller rifles up to .30 caliber. Its usefulness in larger calibers is negated by the increased velocity. Hollow-point ammunition does +2 damage, but only half-normal damage against armored opponents. Wadcutter ammo does +2 damage but base range is reduced by one-half.

Options

Most military firearms are manufactured with a bayonet lug. Effective use of a bayonet requires separate attack and parry skills, both beginning at 20% (Bayonet/Spear skill). Bayonets do 1D8+1+db points of damage and can impale. Some bayonets are small enough to be detached and used as fighting knives.

Telescopic sights allow for precision aim, doubling the base range. Only one shot per round can be fired when taking advantage of this bonus. Similarly, bracing a rifle in the crotch of a tree or other object also doubles the range. Using both methods in conjunction quadruples the range. Note that telescopic sights are delicate and easily knocked out of alignment.

Some Common Rifles

Remington Rolling Block Rifle

First produced in 1867 the Rolling Block design is a simple, rugged, reliable single-shot weapon. Manufactured in numerous calibers until 1934, millions were produced and adopted as standard weapons for the armies of Denmark, Sweden, Norway, Egypt, Spain, and Argentina. Both rifle and carbine versions are available; the military

Remington Rolling Block

A Selection of Rifles

Make/Model	Country	Year	Caliber	Style	Load	Cap	HP	Price
French M1916 Rifle/Carbine	France	1916	8mm Lebel	bolt	clip	5	12/11	$50
Japanese Type 38 Arisaka Rifle/Carbine	Japan	1905	6.5mm Type 38	bolt	clip	5	12/11	$50
Lee-Enfield Mark III Rifle	UK	1907	.303 British	bolt	mag	10	12	$50
Lee-Metford Mark I Rifle/Carbine	UK	1888/1894	.303 Metford	bolt	mag	8/6	12/11	$50
Mannlicher Carcano M1891 Rifle/Carbine	Italy	1891	6.5mm M91-95	bolt	clip	6	12/11	$50
Marlin M1893 Lever-Action Rifle/Carb.ine	USA	1893	.30-30	levr	side	10/7	9/8	$50
Mauser M1893 Rifle/Short Rifle (carbine)	Spain	1893	7mm Mauser	bolt	clip	5	12	$50
Mauser M1898 Rifle/Carbine	Germany	1898	7.92mm Mauser	bolt	clip	5	12/11	$50
Mauser M1903	Turkey	1903	7.65mm Mauser	bolt	clip	5	12	$50
Mauser M1909 Rifle	Argentina	1909	7.65mm Mauser	bolt	clip	5	12	$50
Mauser M1912	Mexico	1912	7mm Mauser	bolt	clip	5	12	$50
Mauser Standard Model 99	Germany	1920	7mm Mau./7.92mm Mau.	bolt	side	5	12	$50
Mau. T-Gewehr M1918 Anti-Tank Rifle	Germany	1918	13mm	bolt	side	1	13	$100
Mondragon M1908 Rifle	Mexico	1908	7mm Mau./7.5mm M11	sel	clip/mag/drum	8/20/30	11	$75
Mosin-Nagant M1891 Rifle/Dragoon (carb.)	Russia	1891	7.62mm Spitzer	bolt	clip	5	12	$50
Remington Rolling Block Rifle	USA	1867	varies	sing	side	1	12	$15-$20
Remington Model 14A Slide-Action Rifle	USA	1912	.25 Rem./.30 Rem./.32 Rem.	pump	side	5	10	$35
Repetier M95 Rifle/Carbine	Austria	1895	8mm M95	bolt	clip	5	12/11	$50
Savage Model 99A Lever-Action Rifle	USA	1899	.30-30/others	levr	side	5	8	$50
Springfield M1903 Rifle	USA	1903	.30-06	bolt	clip	5	12	$50
Schmidt Rubin M1911 Rifle/Carbine	Switzerland	1911	7.5mm M11	bolt	mag	6	12/11	$50
U.S. M1917 Mag 'Enfield' Rifle	USA	1917	.30-06	bolt	clip	5	12	$50
Winchester M1894 Rifle/Carbine	USA	1894	.30-30	levr	side	6/4	9/8	$50
Winchester M1895 Rifle	USA	1895	.30-06/.303 British	levr	side	4/5	9	$50
Winchester Model 54 Rifle	USA	1925	.30-06	bolt	side	5	12	$50

model accepts a bayonet. Modern, smokeless calibers include .22 and .303 British. Remington also produced shotgun versions in 16 and 20-gauge.

Winchester 1895 Carbine

Winchester 1895 Rifle

Winchester M1895 Rifle

This popular model was produced between 1895 and 1931, one of several Winchesters taken by Theodore Roosevelt on his hunting trip to Africa. Of lever-action design, it differs from the usual tubular magazine below the barrel instead using a non-detachable box forward of the trigger guard. This reduces the rifle's capacity to four rounds, five in the .303 British version. Other calibers manufactured include a 7.62mm Spitzer made for the Russian government during the War, the only version incorporating stripper clips.

Barrel lengths include the standard 30, 28, and 24-inch rifle lengths as well as a cumbersome 36-inch long-range version and a 22-inch carbine model. The latter is available only in .30-30, .30-06, and .303 British calibers. Most military versions feature lugs for an 8-inch bayonet.

Mauser M1898 Rifle

Available in both rifle and carbine versions this successor to the M1888 is perhaps the ultimate in bolt-action design. Using the powerful 7.92mm Mauser round, a five-round stripper clip permits quick reloading. The M1898 accommodates any one of several types of bayonets including the notorious saw-backed 'butcher blade.' This weapon was produced in massive quantities and proved as capable of bringing down big game as well as waging war. The basic Mauser design has been copied by many countries.

'Springfield' M1903 Rifle

This rugged, bolt-action rifle, regular issue for U.S troops during the War, was a close copy of the Mauser M1898.

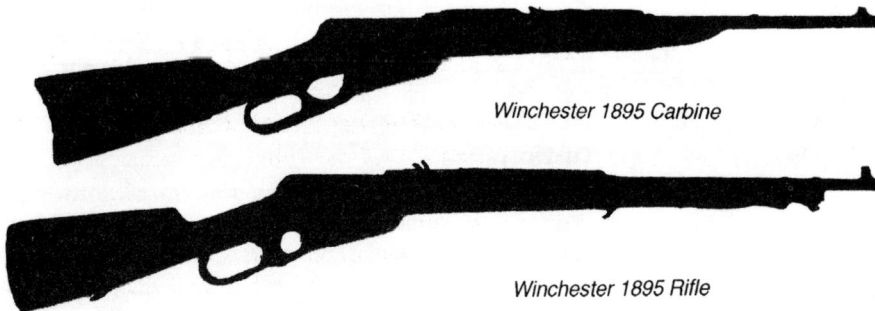

Standard caliber after 1906 was the .30-06 cartridge in a five-round clip. Barrel length is a short 24 inches. These models are still prized by serious marksman.

Lee-Enfield Mark III Rifle

A replacement for the outdated Lee-Metford series, this British rifle uses the .303 British cartridge. Like the Mauser, this rifle features a smooth bolt-action design, but takes advantage of a ten-round magazine for longer firing. The Mark III was the most common Lee-Enfield of the World War.

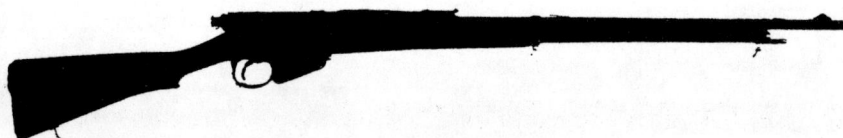

Lee-Enfield Mark III

Mondragon M1908 and M1915 Rifles

The Mondragon is one of the earliest practical semiautomatic rifles. Designed in Mexico by Manuel Mondragon, it was first manufactured by SIG in Switzerland. It was produced in 7mm Mauser for the Mexican Army, and in 7.5mm M11 for Germany.

The M1915 was a selective fire weapon that could be used as a semiautomatic or fully automatic weapon. Aviation versions were equipped with a 30-round drum. A lighter version equipped with a 20-round magazine proved too delicate for the battlefield.

Mauser T-Gewehr Anti-Tank Rifle

Also known as the M1918, this 13mm single-shot, bolt-action rifle is essentially an enlarged version of the standard Mauser military rifle. The first weapon of its type, it packs more than enough punch to penetrate the armor of tanks of the time (25mm and more).

Shotguns

SHOTGUNS ARE DESCENDANTS of primitive fowling pieces, not a part of warfare until the U.S.A. put them to work in the Philippine jungles around the turn of the century. Shotguns are available in sporting, military, and law enforcement versions.

Although having a far shorter range than a rifle, a shotgun takes advantage of firing a load of lead pellets rather than a single slug. Particularly powerful at close range, double-barrel models can fire two charges simultaneously for twice the damage. A shorter barrel increases the tendency of the shot to spread, increasing effectiveness at short range, though at a reduction of long-range effectiveness.

The basic shotgun is a single or double-barrel weapon that breaks open on a hinge for reloading. Lever and pump-action models hold more shells but are more prone to jams. Semiautomatics are also available, requiring no more than a squeeze of the trigger to fire, eject the spent shell, and chamber a fresh round. Shotguns are measured by gauge rather than caliber—the smaller the gauge, the larger and more powerful the shotgun.

Special Ammunition

Different types of shot can be used, ranging from heavy 00 buckshot, to dust-like birdshot. Solid slugs are also available that increase the shotgun's base range. Listed damages for shotguns assume they are loaded with the heaviest shot—usually 00. Weapons used for hunting fowl are loaded with lighter shot. Light birdshot does only half the rolled damage; medium weight shot does three-quarters the rolled damage.

Rock salt ammunition is a favorite among those wishing to inflict painful, but less-than-lethal damage. A rock salt charge does half the normal damage of the weapon; the victim is required to make a CON x5 roll to avoid being incapacitated by painful burning.

Note that the paper casings of normal shotgun shells tend to swell when exposed to wet environments, causing jams in repeating shotguns. Metal-cased shells, though heavy and more expensive, have been available since the end of the Spanish-American War.

Options

Many popular shotguns are produced in so-called 'riot' and 'trench' versions. Riot versions are generally 12-gauge weapons with short barrels, 18-20 inches long. Generally they are pump-action but the lever-action Winchester M1901 and the semiautomatic Remington 11A are both available in riot format.

Trench guns were developed by the U.S. prior to the Great War. Among the first were the Winchester M1897 and M1912, both 12-gauge, slide-action models. Equipped with short, 20-inch barrels and bayonet lugs, they were first made available to the public in 1918. Homemade sawed-off shotguns can have even shorter barrels, further increasing the spread pattern. Stocks are sometimes reduced as well, allowing one to conceal the weapon under an overcoat. When using a short-barrel shotgun, range and chances to hit must be adjusted. For

Some American Shotguns

Make/Model	Year	Gauge	Style	Load	Cap	HP	Price
Greener Far-Killer Model	1893	8/10/12	doub	brek	2	12	$40-45
Ithaca Auto and Burglar Shotgun	1921	20	doub	brek	2	10	$35
Remington M1894 Double Barrel	1894	10/12/16	doub	brek	2	12	$40-45
Remington M1889 Double Barrel	1889	10/12/16	doub	brek	2	12	$40-45
Remington Model 11A	1905	12/16/20	semi	side	5	10	$60
Remington Model 10A	1907	12	pump	side	5	10	$45
Savage Model 620 Slide-Action	1927	12/16/20/.410	pump	side	5	10	$45
Savage Mdl. 720 Autoloader Shotgun	1930	12/16	semi	side	4	10	$60
Winchester M1887 Lever-Action	1887	10/12	levr	side	5	8	$50
Winchester M1897 Slide-Action	1897	12/16	pump	side	5	10	$45
Winchester M1901 Lever-Action	1901	12	levr	side	5	8	$50
Winchester M1911 Self-Loading	1911	12	semi	side	5	10	$60
Winchester M1912 Slide-Action	1912	12/16/20/28	pump	side	5	10	$70

riot and trench guns with 20-inch barrels, reduce base range by one-third and increase chances to hit by 5 points. Shorter barrels can reduce range by as much as one-half, and add 10 points to the chances to hit.

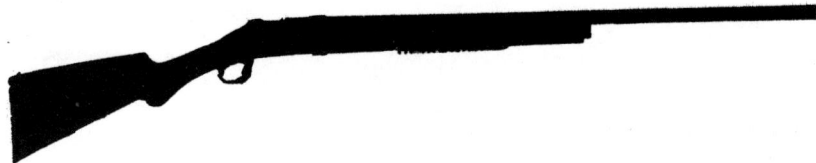

Winchester Slide Action Shotgun

Some Selected Shotguns

Remington M1889

The last in a series that began with the M1883, this double-barrel shotgun with exposed hammers is available in 10, 12, and 16-gauge, with barrel lengths ranging between 28 and 32 inches. When production ceased in 1909 over 37,500 of these firearms had been produced.

Winchester M1887 Shotgun and M1901 Shotgun

This distinctive, lever-action, hammer shotgun was popular despite its strange, even ugly appearance. Two models were produced; the M1887 in 10 and 12-gauge black powder, and the M1901 in 10-gauge smokeless powder. Both feature five-round, tubular magazines. In 1898 both

Winchester Lever Action Shotgun

versions became available in short-barrel riot versions. Non-riot barrel lengths are 30 and 32 inches. Over 75,000 of these shotguns were produced before production ceased in 1920. They are the only 10-gauge Winchesters ever made.

Winchester M1897 Shotgun

Intended as a replacement for the trouble-plagued M1893, this shotgun was a tremendous success. A pump-action, with exposed hammer, over a million were produced between 1897 and 1957. A popular hunting weapon seeing great use in the civilian sector, thousands of trench versions served the military while a riot version was marketed to law enforcement agencies. Hunting versions sport barrel lengths between 26 and 30 inches, while the riot and trench versions are fitted with 20-inch barrels. The trench version features a protective, ventilated barrel jacket and a bayonet lug. Available in 12 or 16-gauge, all M1897s feature 5-round tubular magazines beneath the barrel.

Winchester M1912 Shotgun

This common firearm, a pump-action hammerless design, is available in 12, 16, and 20-gauge (28-gauge in 1934). Riot and trench versions were first produced in 1918. The riot gun is fairly common but after the end of the World War the trench model must be special ordered. The M1912 stays in production until 1980.

Submachine Guns

THE DESIGN OF submachine guns—hand-held fully-automatic weapons—was greatly enhanced by the World War. Usually firing pistol ammunition, many have selector switches allowing them to be used in either semiautomatic or fully automatic mode.

Thompson .45 Submachine Gun

The Italian 9mm Villar Perosa appeared in 1915; the first German Bergmanns did not show up until near the end of the war. The famous Thompson .45 caliber submachine gun first goes on the market in 1921.

High rates of fire call for expanded ammunition capacity. Various sized magazines and drums are used, some holding as many as 50 or 100 rounds. The larger drums are particularly heavy and bulky.

Fully automatic weapons were not regulated at the federal level until 1934. Many private bodyguards, as well as law enforcement agencies, make conspicuous use of Thompsons. They are also a favorite among warring gangsters and bootleggers. Magazine advertisements for the weapon show a cowboy in chaps on horseback, his deadly black Thompson resting across his lap, ready to put a stop to any would-be rustlers.

A Couple Submachine Guns

Bergmann MP18I

This weapon was developed near the end of the War, too late to have any real impact on the outcome. Chambered for 9mm Parabellum, it fired 'automatic only' at a cyclic rate of 350-400 rounds per minute from a 20-round drum magazine. The MP28II is a later version, developed in secret in violation of Germany's surrender conditions. It features minor internal modifications, better sights, and a choice of 20 or 30-round box magazines, or a 32-round 'snail' drum. A selector switch allows a choice of semi-automatic or fully automatic fire.

Thompson M1921

M1921 is a modified version or the original model introduced in 1919. Chambered for the .45 ACP, the 'Tommy gun' uses either 20 and 30-round box magazines, or the more cumbersome 50 and 100-round drums. It has a cyclic firing rate of 800 rounds per minute. The Model 1928 features a horizontal forward grip (in place of the original pistol-grip) and a reduced firing rate of 650 rounds per minute.

Machine Guns

THE FIRST TRULY automatic machine gun was invented in 1884 by Hiram Maxim. Although Gatling guns and other designs had already appeared, the Maxim was the first to use the weapon's energy to eject spent cartridges and rechamber fresh rounds rather

Submachine Guns

Make/Model	Country	Year	Caliber	Style	Load	Cap	HP
Bergmann MP18I	Germany	1918	9mm Parabellum	auto	drum	32	8
Bergmann MP28II	Germany	1928	9mm Parabellum	sel	mag	32	8
Beretta M1918	Italy	1918	9mm Glisenti	sel	mag	25	8
Steyr Solothurn (MP34)	Austria	1930	9mm Mauser/9mm Steyr	auto	mag	32	8
Thompson M1921	USA	1921	.45 ACP	sel	mag/drum	20,30/50,100	8

Machine Guns

Make/Model	Country	Year	Caliber	Action	Load	Cap	HP
Browning M1917A1 (WC-AC)	USA	1917	.30-06	auto	belt	250	12
Browning M1918 Auto. Rifle (AC)	USA	1918	.30-06	sel	mag	20	11
Browning M1921 .50 Cal. (WC-AC)	USA	1921	.50	auto	belt	250	14
Hotchkiss M1914 (AC)	France	1914	8mm Lebel	auto	strp/belt	24/30/250	12
Japanese Type 3 (AC)	Japan	1914	6.5mm Type	38	auto/strp	30	12
Lewis Gun Mark I (AC)	UK	1912	.303 British	auto	drum	47/97	12
Maxim MG08/15 (WC)	Germany	1915	7.92mm Mauser	auto	belt	50/100/250	12
Revelli M1914 (WC)	Italy	1914	6.5mm M91-95	sel	mag	50	12
Vickers (WC)	UK	1912	.303 British	auto	belt	250	12

than manual cranking. By 1895 American inventor John A. Browning had sold to the U.S. Army a model of his own design making use of gas pressure to automatically eject and rechamber cartridges. These two designs encompass the basic principles behind all automatic and semiautomatic weapons.

Machine guns are roughly separated into three groups. Heavy machine guns are tripod-mounted in semipermanent installations or mounted on vehicles, and usually .50 caliber or larger. Medium machine guns are also tripod (or bipod) mounted, but portable, weighing between 25 and 60 pounds. They generally require two men to carry and set up, and although they can be operated by one man, a second man feeding belts reduces the chances of jamming. Although mobile, they are best used as defensive weapons. Light machine guns weigh between 15 and 30 pounds, small enough to be easily carried and deployed by one man. The Browning Automatic Rifle

Browning .30 cal. Machine Gun

(BAR) and the British Lewis Gun both meet these specification.

Some machine guns are water-cooled (WC), though many later designs are air-cooled (AC). Water-cooling requires a special condenser and water container connected to the firearm by hoses. If not properly cooled, these weapons are subject to misfires and jams. The bulk and weight of this additional equipment adds to mobility problems and, combined with the weight of several hun-

dred rounds of ammunition on belts, it is easy to understand why these weapons are best used defensively.

Proven Machine Guns

Mark I Lewis Gun
The Lewis Gun debuted in Belgium in 1913, soon after making its way into the arsenals of England, the U.S., and Japan. Chambered in either .303 British or .30-06 calibers, the fully automatic Lewis gun is fed by a circular drum holding 47 rounds mounted horizontally atop the gun. Although it has a shoulder stock, the Lewis gun's loaded weight of 27 pounds makes its short bipod and a prone firing position almost essential. Lewis Guns are routinely fitted to aircraft, mounted on a swivel and fired by a passenger. These usually dispense with the shoulder stock and opt for the larger, 97-round drum. Firing at a cyclic rate of 450-500 rounds per minute, Lewis Guns are particularly prone to jams.

Browning M1918 Automatic Rifle
The famed BAR debuted in 1918. Chambered for the .30-06 round, it weighs in at an imposing 16 pounds but with the aid of its sling can still be supported and fired from a standing position. A selector switch allows a choice of semiautomatic or full automatic. It carries a 20-round box magazine. A version manufactured in Poland in 1928 is chambered for 7.92mm Mauser ammunition.

Vickers .303 Caliber Machine Gun
Belt-fed and mounted on a heavy tripod, the British Vickers was first introduced in 1912. Firing a .303 cartridge, it has a cyclic rate of 450-500 rounds per minute. Water-

cooled, the early models had a problem with steam rising from around the barrel, obscuring the shooter's vision. Later models corrected this. This weapon features dual spade-handle handgrips, the trigger depressed by the thumbs. A special, air-cooled version is suitable for aircraft only.

Browning .30 cal. with shoulder stock and bipod

Browning M1917 .30 Caliber Machine Gun

Designed to replace the old 1895 Colt-Browning model, this weapon fires a .30-06 cartridge from a 250-round belt at a cyclic rate of 450-600 rounds per minute. Water-cooled, this machine gun features a pistol grip and conventional trigger. The later M1919 is an air-cooled version commonly fitted to aircraft.

Browning M1921 .50 Caliber Machine Gun

Weighing in at 84 pounds (plus a 44-pound tripod), the 65-inch long Browning fires from a 250-round belt at a cyclic rate of 450-575 rounds per minute with a muzzle velocity of 2900 feet per second. Armor piercing ammunition is available. A later version, the M2HB, is air-cooled.

Ammo and Accessories

AMMUNITION FOR THE more common American calibers is easily obtained at hardware and general stores; even large department store outlets have hunting departments.

Pistol and rifle ammunition is usually sold in boxes of 50 or 100 rounds. Selected prices per hundred are: .22 rimfire, 50 cents; .32, $2.59; .30-30, $5.28. .45 Auto, $8.60. Shotgun shells (paper-cased) are priced per hundred as follows: 20-gauge, $3.08; 16-gauge, $3.16; 12-gauge, $3.48; 10-gauge, $3.72; metal-cased shells are approximately three times this price.

Extra ammunition can be carried in a number of different ways. Bandoliers, made of leather or fabric, are belts worn across the torso. Loops tailored to the size of specific cartridges can hold up to 50 or 60 additional rounds. Cartridge belts are similar, but worn round the waist, and may have a place to attach a pistol holster. Bandoliers and cartridge belts range in price from 79 cents to $1.79. A khaki vest with loops for shells costs $1.08. Small magazine pouches holding one to three pre-loaded magazines can be hung on a belt or even a shoulder holster harness. Dump pouches are simple cloth pouches worn around the waist apron-style, holding loose cartridges, preloaded magazines, etc.

Keeping a firearm properly cleaned is essential. Gun cleaning kits designed specifically for your type of firearm are available for $1 or less. Waterproof cases for rifles and shotguns cost $1-$2, while fancier reinforced leather cases complete with brass fittings run $6.59. High-quality sponge rubber recoil pads designed to protect the shoulder cost $2.75.

The serious shooter intent on improving his skills on the range may want to consider reloading his own shells. Retrieving and reloading spent cartridges is an economical way to shoot, and can justify the cost of the equipment. Reloading your own shells also allows you to experiment with different powder loads, slug shapes, etc. ■

Xtra-Range **Xtra-Range**

25 for $1.02

Loads Recommended for Game

Firearms Tables

THE FOLLOWING TABLES provide all the information necessary to generate a complete set of statistics for any weapon chosen from the firearms lists. Additionally, this information can be used to assess the comparative qualities of an unlisted gun, allowing for the assignment of reasonably accurate statistics.

Damage Tables

THE damage done by a bullet depends upon its caliber and the type of weapon used. The shorter barrels of pistols and submachine guns make for lower muzzle velocities and damages are less than equivalent rifle and machine gun calibers. Separate damage tables are given for Handguns and Submachine Guns, and for Rifles and Machine Guns. Shotguns are dealt with on their own separate table.

Handgun & Submachine Gun Damage Table

Caliber	Damage
Small Caliber	
.22 short	1D4
.22 long	1D6
.22 long rifle	1D6+1
.25 ACP	1D6
Medium Caliber	
.32 ACP; Colt Long; rimfire; S&W Long; S&W Short	1D8
.38 Colt; Colt Auto; Super Auto; S&W; Special; Webley	1D10
.380 ACP	1D10
.41 rimfire short	1D10
7.62mm M95; Type P	1D8
7.63mm Mauser	1D8
7.65mm Long; Mannlicher; Mauser	1D8
8mm M1904	1D8
9mm Browning Long; Glisenti; Largo; Mauser; Parabellum; Steyr; Type 26	1D10
Large Caliber	
.41 Colt; rimfire	1D10+1
.357 Magnum	1D8+1D4
.44 Special	1D10+2
.45 ACP; Colt	1D10+2
.455 Webley; Webley Auto	1D10+2

Rifle and Machine Gun Damage Table

Cartridge	Damage
Small Caliber	
.22 short	1D4
.22 long	1D6
.22 long rifle	1D6+1
.25 Remington	1D6+1
.25-20	2D6
Large Caliber	
.30 Remington	2D6+3
.30-30	2D6+3
.30-06	2D6+4
.303 British; Metford	2D6+4
.32 Remington; Special	2D6+3
.35 Remington	2D6+3
.50 M2 (machine gun)	2D10+4
6.5mm M91-95; Type 38	2D6+3
7mm Mauser; M93	2D6+4
7.5mm M11; Rimless	2D6+4
7.62mm Spitzer	2D6+4
7.65mm Mauser	2D6+2
7.7mm Type 99	2D6+4
7.92mm Mauser	2D6+4
8mm Lebel; M35; M95	2D6+4
11mm M71	2D6+4
13mm Mauser (anti-tank rifle)	2D10+4

Base Ranges

Handguns: Standard base ranges for handguns are 10 yards for small calibers, 15 yards for medium and heavy calibers. This assumes a handgun with a more or less standard-length barrel of 4.5 to 5 inches. Pistols with longer barrels—say 7.5 inches—should increase the base range by five yards (such handguns are difficult to conceal). Likewise, shorter barrels result in a decreased base range: 10 yards for a 3-inch barrel, 5 yards for a 1.5-inch barrel. These 'snub-nose' models are very easy to conceal. Derringers and other 'palm guns' have a base range of 3 yards.

Rifles: Standard base ranges for rifles are 40 yards for small calibers; 120 yards for large calibers. Alternatively, you may wish to expand the small caliber range: .22 short, 30 yards; .22 long, 40 yards; .22 long rifle or .25 caliber, 50 yards; .25-20, 80 yards. All ranges assume full-length rifles. Carbines, with their shorter barrels (usually around 18-22 inches) reduce rifle ranges to 3/4 normal.

Shotguns: See Special *Shotgun Damage and Range* table below.

Submachine Guns: Submachine guns use pistol ammunition. Their generally longer barrels give all these weapons a base range of 20 yards.

Machine Guns: Most light and medium machine guns use rifle ammunition and consequently have a base range of 110 yards. .50 caliber machine guns have a base range of 200 yards. Note that these ranges assume proper mounting on bipod or tripod, as required.

Shotgun Damages and Base Ranges

SHOTGUNS can be loaded with either normal shot or rifled slugs. Only slugs are capable of impaling. Ranges assume a normal, sporting length barrel. Riot and trench gun ranges should be reduced by as much as one-third, sawed-off shotguns by one-half or more. Increase chances to hit by 5 or 10 points, respectively. Again, older, black powder weapons have ranges approximately three-quarters the distances given below.

Multiple damage figures are given for weapons using shot, the amount of damage decreasing as distance increases. Figures such as 2D6/10 yards, 1D6/20 yards, 1D3/50 yards indicates that this weapon does 2D6 points of damage up to and including 10 yards away, 1D6 points of damage up to 20 yards, and 1D3 points up to 50 yards. Beyond 50 yards damage is minimal, 1 or 1D2 up to 100 yards, for small and large gauge, respectively.

Gauge	Damage	Base Range
Small Gauge		
.410 slug	1D10+2	40 yards
.410 heavy shot	1D10	10 yards
	1D4	20 yards
	1D4	50 yards
28-gauge slug	1D10+3	35 yards
28-g. buckshot	1D6+1D3	10 yards
	1D4	20 yards
	1D2	50 yards
20-gauge slug	1D10+4	30 yards
20-g. buckshot	2D6	10 yards
	1D6	20 yards
	1D3	50 yards

Shotgun Damages and Base Ranges, continued

Gauge	Damage	Base Range
Large Gauge		
16-gauge slug	1D10+5	30 yards
16-g. buckshot	2D6+2	10 yards
	1D6+1	20 yards
	1D4	50 yards
12-gauge slug	1D10+6	30 yards
12-g. buckshot	4D6	10 yards
	2D6	20 yards
	1D6	50 yards
10-gauge slug	1D10+7	25 yards
10-g. buckshot	4D6+2	10 yards
	2D6+1	20 yards
	1D8	50 yards
8-gauge slug	1D10+8	25 yards
8-g. buckshot	4D6+6	10 yards
	2D6+4	20 yards
	1D10	50 yards

Rate of Fire

RATE of Fire—also called *Attacks per Round*—is the number of well-aimed shots that can be fired by a given weapon within the space of a single round. Recoil and recovery time depends on caliber (small, medium, or large), while rechambering and cocking time are a function of the weapon's particular action. Both affect rate of fire. Handguns and submachine guns are generally quicker than rifles and shotguns.

Note that single-shot weapons can fire only once per round, then need reloading. Double-barrel weapons can empty both chambers simultaneously, or consecutively within the round. A fully automatic weapon can spew 20 bullets within the space of a combat round. Numbers written as 3/2 should be interpreted as three shots fired every two rounds; 1/2 means one shot fired every two rounds; etc.

Two numbers are given for each type weapon. The first number indicates the normal Rate of Fire for most people. If the keeper is agreeable, shooters with skills of 75% or higher may fire at the second, slightly higher Rate of Fire, shown in parentheses.

Handgun and Submachine Gun Rates of Fire

Action/Caliber	Rate of Fire
Single-Action Revolver	
Small Caliber	3/2 (2)
Medium Caliber	1 (1)
Large Caliber	1 (1)
Double-Action Revolver	
Small Caliber	2 (3)
Medium Caliber	3/2 (2)
Large Caliber 1	(3/2)
Semiautomatic	
Small Caliber	3 (4)
Medium Caliber	2 (3)
Large Caliber	1 (2)

Rifle and Shotgun Rates of Fire

Action/Caliber or Gauge	Rate of Fire
Bolt-Action	
Small Caliber	1 (3/2)
Large Caliber	1/2 (1)
Small Gauge	1/2 (1)
Large Gauge	1/2 (1)
Lever-Action	
Small Caliber	2 (2)
Large Caliber	1 (3/2)
Small Gauge	1 (3/2)
Large Gauge	1 (3/2)
Pump-Action	
Small Caliber	2 (3)
Large Caliber	1 (2)
Small Gauge	2 (3)
Large Gauge	1 (3/2)
Semiautomatic	
Small Caliber	2 (3)
Large Caliber	1 (2)
Small Gauge	2 (3)
Large Gauge	1 (3/2)

Reloading Times

Some reloading systems are faster than others. Note that times given for clips, drums, and magazines, as well as belts and strips, assume these devices are preloaded with cartridges. If forced to load the actual clip or detachable magazine, the rate is two cartridges per round. Note that most weapons do not have to be fully reloaded to fire. One or two shots may be all that is needed.

Belt	Two rounds
Break-open	Two cartridges / round
Clip	One round
Drum	One round
Magazine	One round
Side-loading	Two cartridges / round
Strip	One round
Swing-out	Two cartridges / round

Malfunction Table

This table provides general guidelines for firearms malfunctions according to the type of action and the condition of the weapon. The first number listed is for a properly cleaned weapon; the second for a neglected weapon; the third for a very dirty weapon—one that has just been dropped in a mud puddle. This last number may be adjusted to suit exact conditions. Weapons with selector switches malfunction according to whether they are used automatically or semiautomatically.

In most cases a roll of 00 indicates a misfire round. Any other malfunction roll indicates a jammed weapon. Dud rounds pose little problem with revolvers or other manual actions, however, they stop semiautomatics and automatics cold. A Firearms roll for that particular type weapon is required to safely clear a jam. A dud can be cleared in one round, without rolls.

Action	Clean	Neglected	Dirty
Automatic	98	95	70
Bolt-Action	00	00	90
Lever-Action	99	98	85
Pump-Action	99	98	85
Revolver	00	00	96
Semiautomatic	99	97	75
Single-Shot	00	00	95

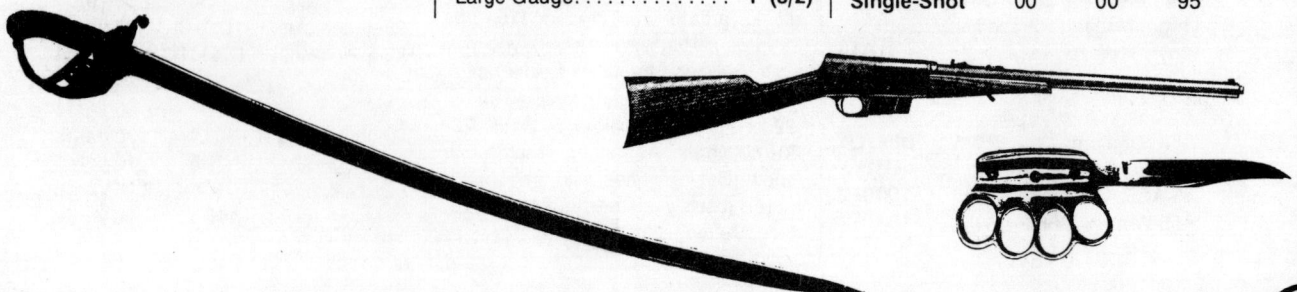

Stock your wardrobe this summer with cool Cthulhu fashion tees. The design shown below is printed on a 100% cotton, black shirt in four mythos colors. Available in sizes up to XXXXL (count 'em). You'll find ordering information on the other side of this page.

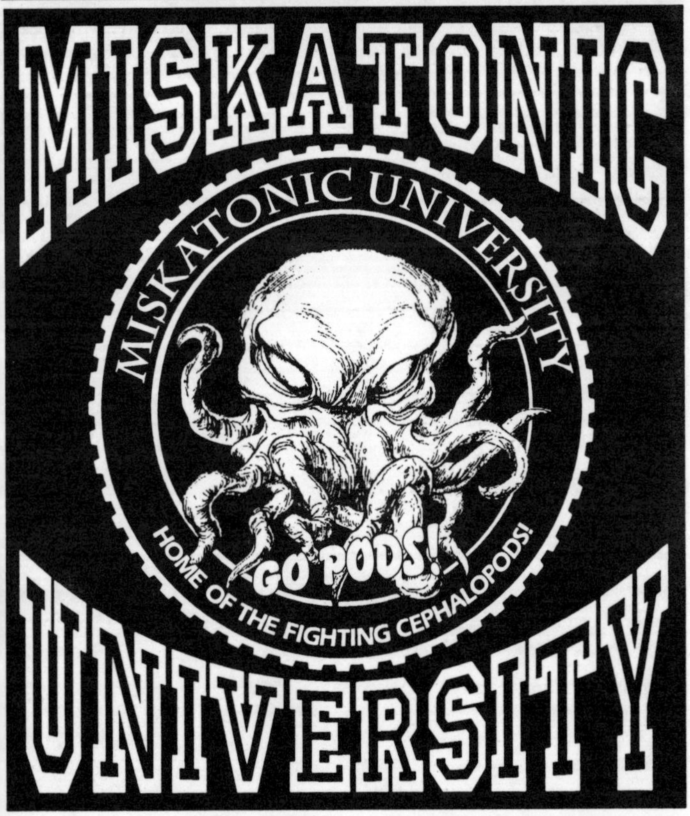

MISKATONIC
MISKATONIC UNIVERSITY
GO PODS!
HOME OF THE FIGHTING CEPHALOPODS!
UNIVERSITY

Chaosium Licensees

The following companies produce licensed products based on our games. If you are interested, write to them for a catalog of their products.

CTHULHU MINIATURES

RAFM CO., INC.
20 PARKHILL RD. EAST
CAMBRIDGE, ONT. N1R 1P2 CANADA

PENDRAGON MINIATURES

LANCE & LASER MODELS, INC.
P.O.BOX 14491
COLUMBUS, OH 43214

FOREIGN LANGUAGE EDITIONS

FRENCH — CALL OF CTHULHU, ARKHAM HORROR, FIELD GUIDES

JEUX DESCARTES
1 RUE DU COLONEL PIERRE AVIA
75503 PARIS CEDEX 15, FRANCE

FRENCH — STORMBRINGER

ORIFLAM
132, RUE DE MARLEY
57158 MONTIGNY LES METZ
FRANCE

GERMAN — PENDRAGON

FANTASY PRODUCTIONS
POSTFACH 260 165
4000 DUSSELDORF 1, GERMANY

GERMAN — CALL OF CTHULHU, STORMBRINGER

LAURIN GMBH
LURUPER CHAUSSEE 125
D-2000 HAMBURG 50,
GERMANY

ITALIAN — CALL OF CTHULHU

STRATELIBRI SRL.
VIA PAISIELLO NO. 4
20131 MILANO, ITALY

JAPANESE — MANY TITLES

HOBBY JAPAN CO, LTD.
5-26-5 SENDAGAYA
SHIBUYA-KU TOKYO, 151
JAPAN

SPANISH — CALL OF CTHULHU, STORMBRINGER, PENDRAGON

JOC INTERNACIONAL
SANT HIPÒLIT
08030 BARCELONA, SPAIN

RUNEQUEST

THE AVALON HILL GAME CO.
4517 HARFORD RD.
BALTIMORE, MD 21214

HI CHAOSIUM,

I just bought your INVESTIGATORS' COMPANION. Please send me your latest info and put me on your mailing list for future announcements of new games, books, and supplements.

NAME ______________________________

ADDRESS ______________________________

CITY/STATE/ZIP ______________________________

I also have a friend who would like to receive your free announcements:

NAME OF FRIEND ______________________________

HIS/HER ADDRESS ______________________________

CITY/STATE/ZIP ______________________________

Please list the complete name and address of the store in which you bought this book:

NAME OF LOCAL STORE ______________________________

ADDRESS ______________________________

CITY/STATE/ZIP ______________________________

HOW DO YOU LIKE THIS BOOK? ______________________________

HOW COULD WE IMPROVE IT? ______________________________

YOUR AGE: ❑ 1-11, ❑ 12-14, ❑ 15-18, ❑ 19-25, ❑ 26-35, ❑ 36+

YOUR OCCUPATION: ❑ student, ❑ blue collar, ❑ white collar, ❑ professional, ❑ other: ______________________________

WHERE DID YOU HEAR OF THIS GAME: ❑ friend, ❑ game convention, ❑ magazine article, ❑ magazine advertisement, ❑ book, ❑ hobby store, ❑ Chaosium flier or catalog, ❑ cosmic vibrations, ❑ other: ______________

Chaosium Inc. Order Form

950-A 56th St. Oakland CA 94608

QUANTITY	ITEM	PRICE	TOTAL

CA residents add appropriate sales tax for your county:

Shipping & Handling: $5.00

VISA,M/C

TOTAL:

CHARGE # ______________________________

EXP DATE ______________ DAY PHONE# ______________

SIGNATURE ______________________________

❑ **Please DO NOT ship by UPS**

NAME ______________________________

ADDRESS ______________________________

CITY/STATE ______________________________ ZIP ______________